BUCK FEVER

Also by Cynthia Chapman Willis

DOG GONE

BUCK FEVER

Cynthia Chapman Willis

FEIWEL AND FRIENDS
NEW YORK

A Feiwel and Friends Book
An Imprint of Macmillan

 Printed in September 2009 in the United States of America by R.R. Donnelley & Sons Company, Harrisonburg, Virginia. For information, address Feiwel and Friends, 175 Fifth Avenue, New York, N.Y. 10010.

Library of Congress Cataloging-in-Publication Data

Willis, Cynthia Chapman.
Buck fever / by Cynthia Chapman Willis. — 1st ed.
p. cm.
Summary: Twelve-year-old Joey's dad expects him to carry on the family tradition of hunting. The family, already strained by the mother's extended travel, is pushed further apart by the father's disappointment that Joey is more interested in drawing deer than hunting them.
ISBN: 978-0-312-38297-1
[1. Family problems—Fiction. 2. Hunting—Fiction. 3. Artists—Fiction. 4. Fathers and sons—Fiction. 5. Brothers and sisters—Fiction. 6. Communication—Fiction. 7. Recluses—Fiction.] I. Title. PZ7.
W6826Buc 2009 [Fic]—dc22 2008034748

Book design by Barbara Grzeslo

Feiwel and Friends logo designed by Filomena Tuosto

First Edition: 2009

10 9 8 7 6 5 4 3 2 1

www.feiwelandfriends.com

This book is dedicated, with lots and lots of love,
to my nephews, Derek and Andrew Kopf.

BUCK FEVER

CHAPTER 1

THE FIRST DAY

"Up by six a.m. Impressive, Joey. Especially for a Saturday." Dad's voice is rough and rocky, but pleased. I'd smile if I had the energy. I don't. Not this early. Not with what I've got to do today.

One of Dad's big hands rubs at the dark grit on his cheeks and chin as he hovers over the gurgling coffeemaker. This unshaven look is weird for him. And his eyelids seem thick. They're drooping. The blue-sky brightness usually under them is clouded over. He doesn't fit into our small, cheery kitchen this morning. This room that is covered in Mom's fingerprints, from the cabinets that she painted white to the walls that she painted milky yellow to the border of teapots and sunflowers that she pasted close to the ceiling. But her mug with the kitten face isn't by her place at the table. Neither is a tea bag or a pad of paper with her scribbled list of things to do.

Our fat, smoke-gray cat arches his back as he rubs against the denim of Dad's left calf, his limping leg. For the first time maybe ever, Dad ignores him, doesn't massage the cat's triangle ears or scratch the base of his tail. Weird again. Dad must have what he calls a "swampy head," again. He doesn't sleep when Mom is away for more than five days.

"We've got a good start to your first day of hunting. Our first day of hunting together." He straightens and turns to me, six feet, two inches of broad and strong. A real grin pushes into his face. "I can't think of anything else that I'd rather be doing today, buddy." He slaps me on my shoulder. I almost spit beef jerky. My breakfast.

This is the kind of enthusiasm that Dad usually shows Philly, my fifteen-going-on-twenty sister, when she breaks track records and wins races. Last year, when she beat one of his best times in a race, he smirked, walked taller, and shoulder-smacked everyone for a full week.

"I've been looking forward to us hunting as a team since the day that you were born."

That's twelve years of anticipation. Even though the words *I'd rather be sleeping* form in my mouth, I don't let them out. I don't tell him how much I've been dreading the next thirteen days—antlered deer season. A once-a-year opportunity to shoot a buck.

The musky cologne that he's wearing hints of Mom's clean linen perfume and reminds me of another reason why I am up and keeping quiet. Mom told Philly (who told me) that Dad mixes a drop of her perfume into his splash of cologne when he's missing her. To keep her close.

He needs the distraction and companionship of our hunting together.

So I force a lame grin and slide my butt onto the yellow cushion of the chair I usually sit in. A bowl of sugared rice cereal in front of me crackles. Since the dread in my gut would curdle the milk, I pull out another strip of beef jerky from my back pocket. Nothing says good morning better than salt-cured, dried meat. Of course, my salad-obsessed mom wouldn't agree. She'd have a heart attack if she knew that this was my breakfast. But she's been gone for nine days, ten hours on her fourth trip in three months, not that I am counting.

When the coffee machine sputters to a stop, Dad snatches the pot. He pours steaming black into his WORLD'S BEST DAD mug, but too fast. Coffee splashes onto the counter, onto his latest history and hunting magazines, which sit on top of junk mail and bills, and onto Philly's nail polish bottles and hoop earrings. When Mom is away, my sister leaves her girl junk all over.

"You and me, hunting buddies, carrying on the MacTagert tradition the way my pop and I did. The way he and his dad did. The way your great-grandfather and his father did." Dad lifts his mug in a toast to me. "Now it's you and me, a team. We'll have memories to treasure for a lifetime, Joey. I loved hunting with my dad."

"Yes, sir." I try to sound excited, try to snuff the dread that is crawling around inside me.

Instead of waiting for the coffee to cool, Dad sips in loud slurps. Black drips onto his green flannel shirt, but he doesn't grab a sponge to wipe at this or the mess on the counter. I stop chewing jerky. Sloppiness isn't in my father. *If it's not health inspection clean, it's not clean enough,* he's said a million times.

If Mom saw this kitchen, she'd hang Dad, my sister, and me. In that order.

When he makes more loud, coffee-sucking noises, I bunch up my face at him, imagining the bitter, molten-tar java frying the inside of his mouth. "Man, Dad, that's got to be blistering your tongue."

"Drinking it scorching is the only way to get it down when I make it." He sticks out his tongue. An *ack* sound comes up from his throat. "No one makes coffee the way your mother does." He slurps again, crinkles his face, and makes another gagging noise as he limps to the cabinet where Mom keeps the vitamins and aspirins. And his jelly beans.

His bum leg is stiffer than usual this morning. The gory details of how he messed it up are a secret. All I know is that a Harley-Davidson motorcycle was involved—the one that he sold as a wedding present to Mom.

"Yes, we'll remember this day forever." He grabs the aspirin bottle, topless since he whipped the childproof cap into the backyard last September. Hours after he'd kicked the tires on his truck and called them pieces of crap. Only a day after he'd shredded the wall calendar on which Mom had marked the weeks when she'd be gone. This wouldn't have been a big deal except that he never used to lose his temper. And my mom had only been gone one week.

That afternoon, Philly and I labeled his hibernating anger "the bear." These days, "the bear is out of its cave" is code for "Dad's anger is out and on the move." That's when inanimate objects get beat up and yelled at. That's when Claude dives for cover.

"Today will be different from all the other times we've been in the woods, son." Chalky tablets clatter into Dad's big palm. They disappear down his throat in a blink, chased by coffee.

I consider asking him to pass the bottle.

He barely puts it down before hobbling into the hunting room, a space off of our kitchen that should be, according to Mom, a dining room. It is the only place in our ranch-style home that she hasn't wallpapered, painted, carpeted, and decorated with furniture and knickknacks that she has bought at yard sales and flea markets. For years Dad has talked about building her the perfect dining room, but so far Mom's dream room is exactly that—a dream.

When Dad returns to the kitchen, he drops boots and an olive-green jacket onto a chair seat. He attaches a nine-inch hunting knife, in its sheath, to his belt. "Today we won't just search out deer paths and food sources, or simply watch the habits of bucks. Today is the hunt."

He grabs his fluorescent-orange vest from the back of another chair and pulls the sleeveless thing over his camouflage tan-and-brown jacket while stepping to my right. As usual. If you ask me, he doesn't want to even glimpse the hearing aid crammed into my left ear. To him, it's an advertisement that his only son has a defect. No, he's never said this. And Philly accuses me of having sniffed glue when I mention it, but the "fifth" in Joseph Morgan MacTagert the fifth means I'm supposed to be a copy of my father, the next in a long line of Joseph Morgan MacTagerts, all hunters.

"Call me sentimental, but I can't stop myself." He picks up the stiff green jacket. It's frayed at the cuffs, worn hard at the elbows, and big enough to cover at least two of me. "For you, son." His free hand pats my shoulder again. And then he picks up the gnarled and scarred ankle-high boots. "I wore this coat and these boots on my first hunt with your grandfather. When I was your age. When I shot my first buck."

"Thanks, Dad." I stand, try to come off as thrilled at being given these things. This isn't easy. The jacket and the boots highlight that I'm not as big as Dad was at twelve. Having a five-foot-no-inches son weighing in at eighty-five pounds (wearing every sweatshirt I own) and sporting a hearing aid has to disappoint him. Philly is already five six.

"Your mother laughed when I told her that I wanted to

give you these." For a moment, his smile is loud, the way it gets when he mentions her. "I told her that wearing your old man's jacket and boots for the first season is a MacTagert tradition." He gives me a wink. "Besides, I thought you'd get a kick out of wearing these."

He drops the boots. Even their thud sounds too big. When he pushes the jacket at me, I get more of a gamy stench than a kick. The thing reeks of dead rodent. The ear infections that ate away at my hearing when I was seven left me with a high-powered nose. Strange, but true, and sometimes really inconvenient.

Dad runs a hand through his thick chestnut hair. This, at least, I inherited from him. Except that his is short and neat while mine is weeks overdue for a cut.

In one step he returns to the coffeemaker. He refills his mug. "Meet me by the truck. Okay, buddy? Two minutes." He snaps off a playful salute and is gone.

Claude jumps onto the table. He sticks his face into the cereal bowl, laps milk as if this were part of his morning routine. For the record, it is not.

I bolt back to my bedroom and pull on four random socks that don't come close to matching. I grab two sweatshirts from the scattered land mines of crumpled clothes all over the floor. After sock sliding back into the kitchen, I stick my overpadded feet into Dad's boots. Even laced up, they still wobble. Cinder blocks tied to my feet would be easier to maneuver.

Next, I throw on Dad's jacket. It hangs over my layers of sweatshirts. By the time I crawl into the blaze-orange hunting vest that Dad bought for me a month ago, I'm doing a great imitation of a deflated blimp that stinks of roadkill.

Cold, raw, beginning-of-December air hits my face as I step outside. Streaked pinks and oranges are just pushing up into the sky, shoving out the dark purples and navy blues. As I open the door on the passenger's side of Dad's black SUV, he throws it into reverse. Mr. Anxious, whistling an old Rolling Stones song playing on the radio—the tune about getting no satisfaction.

"We've got a great morning," he says. "Buckle up."

"We've got a freezing morning." I climb into the cab, into the overpowering odor of fake orange blossoms coming off the cardboard air freshener dangling from the rearview mirror. This sticky smell is not mixing well with the roasted nut aroma of Dad's coffee. Mom gave him this air freshener when she returned from her business trip to Florida. I'm not sure, but I don't think a grinning orange with a painted-on twinkle in its eye screams "I missed you." Still, Dad won't yank the thing down.

As I snap the seat belt together at my hip, the back of my hand brushes crisp fabric. Hunting gloves. The plastic thread holding them together is tangled with the tag of a fluorescent-orange hat. My eyes, brown like Mom's, shift to Dad's face. I tip my head at the gifts. "Thanks."

He gives me another smile. It almost makes getting up too early worthwhile.

Gravel crunches on packed dirt as Dad backs the truck out of our short driveway. The woods aren't far, but I'm glad Dad prefers to drive there. I shiver and shove my hands into the pockets of the hunting jacket. Between all the extra canvas and my layered sweatshirts, I can barely bend my arms.

"You'll get used to the cold once you wake up."

The chill of the hockey rink never bothers me. If I thought I'd be spending the day icing pucks, turning them into oversize bullets shooting across a rink, I wouldn't be thinking about the cold. Dad doesn't get this hockey love. Not even a little. He never has. Skating, chasing a rubber puck, living to slice the thing past a goalie and into a net. All of this is lost on him. *Fine for Canadians,* he's told me more than once. *But hunting is better for kids from Pennsylvania. Once you experience the thrill of shooting a deer, you'll forget about hockey.*

He straightens the truck, guides it down Mercer Place. "Hunting is the MacTagert way. It's in your blood, son."

What if it isn't *this* MacTagert's way? I mean, I'm the kid who stays clear of the backyard when Dad hangs a gutted deer from the trees (to let the carcass bleed out). I'm the MacTagert who flipped out in Mom's car when a squirrel bolted in front of us, too late for her to stop. For weeks I couldn't erase the replay of that fuzzy-tailed rodent sprinting for its nut-loving life before becoming the middle of a tire-rubber-and-asphalt sandwich.

Do I have to become a hunter because MacTagerts have hunted in Pennsylvania since forever? Did the first Joseph Morgan MacTagert go screwy over dead squirrels and carved-out deer in the 1700s? Probably not.

As we come to the end of Mercer Place, where it butts up against County Road 523, I am happy for the distraction that is the house that sits across the two-lane street. The Buckner place, 77 County Road 523. A tall, old, ivory-sided building with sage-green trim and shutters. Mom drools over this house, calls it a "Victorian." I call it creepy. Because the doors are always sealed shut. The windows are never cracked open behind the heavy shades. The black-iron fence that surrounds the place warns all living things to back off. Its gate has been threaded shut with a thick chain and a huge silver padlock since Mrs. Buckner died this past August. Tommy Jackson, my best friend, also known as Jacks, swears the woman was one hundred and ten.

Behind the Buckner gate and fence, the grass is always cut. The bushes and hedges around the front porch are always trimmed. The snow is always shoveled off of the driveway and the cement walkway from the gate to the porch. Fine. Except that no one has ever been seen mowing, trimming, shoveling, or sweeping. People claim to have heard the whirring blades of a lawn mower, the rapid-fire *click-click-click* of a hedge clipper, and the muffled strain of a snowblower blasting away on the Buckner property, but only at night.

I'd kill to hear a lawn mower, clipper, or blower. More than once I've left my hearing aid in, especially on snowy nights, hoping, always hoping.

As I stare, I gasp the way a girl would. A knee-jerk reaction that I hope Dad didn't catch. When he doesn't tease me about this, I point at the lights on a tall pine by the corner of the porch. More bulbs speckle the bushes near the steps. "Someone hung holiday lights!"

"It's that time of year," Dad comments. As if new lights are no big deal. As if they don't prove that Mr. and Mrs. Buckner's adult son, M. K., *is* still living inside that house. People say he is a sixty-something Vietnam War veteran. A big guy, made mostly of muscle. And scary crazy.

According to talk, M. K. Buckner joined the United States Army Rangers—an elite, special operations force of the army—and did two tours of duty in Vietnam. Supposedly the guy became a trained sniper. Everyone agrees that he ended up being awarded a Bronze Star medal for being heroic and a Purple Heart after being wounded, but some say M. K. Buckner also snapped. They say all the jungle warfare, death, and destruction pushed him over the edge.

"Jacks swears M. K. Buckner only comes out at night," I blurt out.

"You know how I feel about gossip, son."

But Jacks doesn't spread rumors. He had nothing to do

with the latest whispers about M. K. Buckner strangling his mother and burying her under the front porch steps of 77 County Road 523. This story started the day after Mrs. Buckner died, when the town woke up to find piles of loose dirt where the porch steps had been. Three days later, new steps had replaced the dirt. But no one saw anyone doing any demolition or rebuilding. There was never a funeral.

As usual, I'm itching to ask Dad about the other rumors, too. Especially the one about M. K. Buckner prowling the woods at night as his special ops killing-machine self. Does he relive old war battles in flashbacks? Another of my pals, Steve Katz, a kid into all things military, says M. K. could be reliving past hunter-killer missions—operations that the Rangers executed in Vietnam.

Whenever I hear this, a seven-foot monster man in green camouflage storms into my head. My knees almost give out as I picture his face painted in shades of green that make the whites of his eyes glow with pure crazy. My stomach double-knots as I imagine a nine-and-a-half-inch bowie knife clenched between his teeth.

I'm almost desperate to ask Dad whether it's true that M. K. Buckner once killed a hunter. A poor sap who didn't get out of the woods before sunset. This would explain why some kids say that M. K. stands for "Man Killer." But asking about this will get me a lecture on the value of minding my own business.

"The Buckners have always kept to themselves. You

know that, son," Dad reminds me. "Michael Buckner is a patriot and a veteran who gave more for this country in a few years than most people give in their lifetimes." Dad's voice is no-nonsense, the way it gets when he discusses love of country. "The man deserves compassion and respect. Gossip is for bullies." Dad yanks the truck right, onto 523.

"Yes, sir," I agree.

"Now, let's concentrate on your big day," Dad adds.

"What if I'm not ready? What if I need more target practice?" Dad and I have a blast plinking, or shooting at nonliving targets, together. The second he showed me how to hold a gun, three years ago, I understood his fascination with how it worked, how it had to be handled, and why its power should be understood and respected. *Shooting is a combined challenge that requires keeping a gun steady while aiming, lining up a thing to be shot, and then squeezing the trigger at the exact right instant, all while fighting the impulse to tense up,* he told me.

The satisfaction of doing everything right at once means hitting a target. For me, that's blowing the cotton and fiber out of one of Philly's old stuffed animals or putting a bullet into one of her retired dolls. Like Dad, I love the sweet smoke aroma of spent gunpowder. I could target shoot forever. Old toys don't have heartbeats. They don't feel pain.

"You're ready to hunt," Dad says. "You've hit every target I've put out, dead on."

Did he have to say "dead"?

"You've got my eye." He winks at me. "Believe me, if

you weren't a natural, we'd only be going after rabbit today. If that." Dad sips more coffee. "Don't worry."

Don't worry? I might as well not breathe.

"Maybe you'll get a shot at Old Buck today." Dad lifts his mug in another toast to me. "Wouldn't that be something?"

"It would be something, all right." Flying to Mars would be something, too, but I don't see myself doing that.

"There's not a serious hunter in all of eastern Pennsylvania or western Jersey that wouldn't love to line up Old Buck in his or her gun sights."

As if I don't know this. Old Buck is a celebrity. Over two hundred pounds, he's big for a white-tailed deer. And he grows a fine rack of antlers each season. Usually twelve points, six points or better on each side. I know. I track Old Buck a lot. But not to shoot him.

"Some say he's the smartest white-tailed deer in the Northeast," I add. The closest he ever got to being a trophy shows on his face—a furless, diagonal streak across his forehead. A scar, the story goes, traced by a hunter's bullet.

"Nothing would make me more proud than for you to shoot that deer," Dad tells me.

There it is. "Proud," I repeat, the word thick and sticky in my mouth.

"No pressure." Dad gives me a grin and turns the truck onto Mill Road.

I sink into the seat, trying not to picture Old Buck's carcass hanging from a tree in our backyard. For a split second, I consider (for the six billionth time) telling Dad that I don't think I can shoot a living thing. But I say zip (for the six billionth time). I can't disappoint him. Again.

CHAPTER 2

SATURDAY

Too soon Dad pulls the truck up and onto the grass bank across from the opening to Dewey's field, which butts up against the woods where Dad has been hunting for five years, since Mr. Dewey gave him almost exclusive access to the private property. Only Mr. Cheetavera (the father of my pal, Cheets) and one other man, who Dad tells me I don't know, have permission to hunt here.

"Let's hope that one of us brings down a whitetail today. We could use the meat."

That's my dad. He uses every bit of the animals that he shoots and usually donates deer meat to food banks and homeless shelters.

"Even a rabbit wouldn't be bad to begin with." He tips back his mug, gulps the last of his coffee. And then he grabs the brown lunch bag sitting on the dashboard. He rolls the paper top over the jelly beans and slides the bag into his jacket pocket. "Okay, Joey. Let's go." He hops out of the truck.

After snapping the tags off the hat and gloves, I pull the fleece stocking cap over my bed-head hair. I stuff the gloves into the side pockets of the jacket. Ready as I'll ever be, I push myself out of the truck. My feet jiggle in Dad's boots as they hit the hard ground. Something in my gut curdles, leaving a cottage cheesy ick that's hard to ignore. Still, I trudge through the thick mist that clings to the tall, dried grasses and pushes its cold fingers under my layers of clothing.

Moving to the back of the Jeep, Dad sucks in this morning air through his nose. His chest puffs out as he holds this breath in for a count of about ten Mississippis. And then he lets it out. "There's nothing as energizing as a crisp autumn morning, the sweet smells of decaying leaves and fresh mud, the aging bark, and the feel of a well-made weapon." Dad's breath is a fog.

I nod as he pulls the earflaps down on his orange thermal hat. Next, he opens the back door of the Jeep and picks up Granddad's gun. Dad's been letting me use it since my twelfth birthday, last April. Still, he pushes the .30 caliber, lever-action rifle toward me with slow and careful respect, as if he's handing it to me for the first time. His expression is lifted, proud.

"I wish your grandfather could be here. Some of my best memories are of hunting with him when I was your age."

That's when I think I smell deer. A scent that is one part horse and one part musky wild thing with a sweet edge of grass and clover. "I wish Granddad was here, too," I say as I accept his rifle. For the first time, it feels cold, awkward, and unfriendly in my hands, different from when I am target shooting.

After Dad lifts his own gun, also a .30 caliber, lever-action rifle, he reaches into his jacket pocket and pulls out six bullet-shaped cartridges. "Here you go." He pushes them at me.

They land heavy in my palm. Each cartridge holds its own bullet and charge. With decent aiming, one of these bullets could tear into the soft tissue of a deer and stop its heart. My aim is good. If I stay steady, I could snuff a life in an instant with one of these cartridges.

My hands turn clammy.

Still, I imitate Dad and pull the rod from the front of Granddad's rifle. I drop the cartridges, one at a time, into the gun. And then I slide the rod in after them.

Done.

Dad chambers a round in his own rifle. The cartridge clicks and moves up into the barrel, making the gun ready to fire. His thumb moves to the hammer, slowly slides it forward. Now the gun can't go off until he pulls the hammer back again, when he pinpoints a target.

Locked and loaded, Dad scans the field, which is

washed in the tangerine light of the sun peeking over the horizon. "This way," he commands, pushing through the grasses, heading toward the thin deer path that we've followed a million times, a Bambi highway into the tall shadows of the sycamores and shaggy pines. Welcome to Dewey's woods.

"I know you're itching to fire at a live target," Dad says. He applies another clap to my back. "But remember, the key to hunting is to stay calm and to be steady."

Calm? Not the way my heart is galloping. Steady? Not in Dad's oversize boots.

His hand dives into his pocket. The brown bag crinkles. He pulls out a rainbow of jelly beans, tosses a few of them into the air, and catches them in his mouth. He does this a lot, but I'm always impressed. "Do we need to go over my hunting rules again?" Dad's free hand moves to his left side. Whenever he mentions laws or rules, he touches his bum leg.

"Always know your target and what is beyond it," I recite. "Never shoot unless you're sure of a kill. And never hunt alone."

Dad nods his approval. "And?"

"Never cross a fence or barrier without disarming your weapon. Always unload it."

"Good." Dad tosses, catches, and chews more jelly beans as we step into the shade of the trees. "On my first day of hunting with your granddad, I shot a four-point buck."

There it is. The expectation. "Yeah," I say. "You've mentioned that." Two, maybe three hundred times.

He winks at me. "No pressure," he says again.

He's got to be kidding.

Dad slows, begins his stalk. No more jelly beans. He slides around wispy trees and ducks under the thick branches of older ones. He avoids shriveled leaves that rattle. He squints at bark, inspects it for antler scrapes. He squats to analyze the deer path for fresh tracks and droppings.

I don't tell him that we're light-years away from deer. The scent that I picked up back in the field has evaporated. Now my nose detects only half-frozen mud and rotting leaves. Until one of Dad's boots launches a can, sends it flying. The thing lets go the sharp, sour stink of stale beer as it *pings* against a rock.

Two long, no-nonsense strides bring Dad to that rock. He snatches the can. As it dribbles gold, his jaw hardens. His lips press together. His eyes shrink into a squint. "Beer. I'd better not catch anyone drinking out here or littering in these woods." He drops the can and crushes it under his boot. "Responsible hunters care about the environment."

"Yes, sir." I nod.

He picks up the aluminum wad and stuffs it into the side pocket of his camouflage jacket. "Wooded areas are refuges from the world of concrete and asphalt. We can't allow them to be destroyed." He stomps off.

I keep quiet, the way I do whenever a conversation turns toward progress and what Dad calls "suburban encroachment." He hates the new homes, malls, and condos that have been filling the fields where he and his buddies once roamed. The worst, he says, was losing Duke's field to the hockey rink and its parking lot.

As I follow him, a thin wisp of deer floats over from my right and drifts under my nose.

"I'd better not find any traps, either," Dad mutters. As much as he is into hunting, he is anti-trap. Wounding animals, leaving them to suffer and die from the bite of metal teeth, is unacceptable to him.

"Here we are." He picks up his pace when he spots the mottled brown, gray, and tan tentlike blind that he has surrounded with brush. He has positioned it close to the deer path and two young red maples that are candy to whitetails. "I've already sprayed the blind with deer scent," he whispers. No kidding.

Velcro rips as Dad pulls back the entrance flap of the blind and pushes through the opening. At the back wall, he places the front end of his rifle barrel through the small shoot-through window. I copy his moves, set up in the same way at the side of the tent. But unlike Dad, who is peering out the window, on high alert, his muscles twitching and his expression close to a grin, I swallow back a dense sigh. Something tells me that this is going to be a long day. The oily, skunklike stink of the deer scent is starting to make me see double and is not reacting well with my jerky breakfast. Cold is gnawing on my fingertips and scratching with frozen claws at my nose. All this along with the heavy dread of what could happen today.

Bone-chilling, deer-less hours inch by. After the first hour, my neck cramps and I start wrestling with a serious need to fidget. I struggle to stay poised, ready, and as quiet as possible, the way Dad does. Since deer have sharp hearing and a decent sense of smell, Dad isn't moving and isn't chewing jelly beans. By the second hour, Granddad's gun grows heavy, heavier, heaviest. My muscles start to whine. My feet go numb. I try to stretch without Dad noticing. I'd give a month of allowance to hear him say *Let's go home, buddy*.

"Hunting can be a waiting game," he whispers.

Yeah, a game that's about as entertaining as watching Philly's nail polish dry.

After another hour slug-crawls by, Dad staying poised while I'm about to do an impression of a Mexican jumping bean, he glances my way. "I'm surprised we haven't seen any animals. There must be a deer convention on the other side of Bucks County."

"Deer convention?" I shake my head. "Real lame, O

King of the Bad Jokes." But I almost add a thanks for his attempt at trying to lighten the pressure. "If we were tracking deer, at least we'd be moving."

Dad jerks back from the window and turns to me. His blue eyes almost shine. "You're right." He swells, seems ready to spring to his feet, which would wreck the five-foot-high blind. "Why didn't I think of that?" He rubs his forehead. "I'm not thinking straight."

Meaning that he's got Mom on his mind.

"Come on, son." He exits the blind as if his jeans have caught on fire.

Once I'm out, he steps aside to let me lead. This makes me feel important.

"Where to, son?"

I hesitate. Breathe in the smells of the woods. "Right," I say, starting along the Bambi path. Behind me, Dad chews another quick handful of jelly beans. My nose picks up deer behind the black licorice.

"I still can't get over your tracking abilities," he whispers. "My granddad used to talk about how his dad could track a deer. Maybe you've inherited this ability."

I shrug as a feather breeze brings me a more concentrated deer scent. I follow it, lead Dad through the cluster of five birches. At the edge of a clearing, sweat pricks at the back of my neck even though I'm the approximate temperature of a snow cone. Yeah, I've been to this place at least fifty times. Dad doesn't know why and I don't want him to know, but I've spent hours with my butt on the old stone wall at the other side of the meadow. Watching Old Buck.

Dad moves close to my good ear. "Look! Across the meadow." His pointing finger is rigid. "Two doe. One buck." Excitement cracks his whisper. "That buck is all yours, son."

The trees whisper, but the birds go quiet. On the outside I don't move, but my insides start to quiver. My palms go slick, but I still manage to pull the lever of Granddad's rifle. *Click.* A cartridge slides into the chamber. Dad's tension turns the air electric. Yeah, I should have had a round already in the chamber.

The buck lifts his four-point antlers. His nostrils flare. His ears become stiff. Concern fills his large almond eyes. It's a look that bites into my chest.

"Aim for his heart," my father whispers.

A heart or lung shot is clean and brings a deer right down. No suffering, no running off wounded. No dying of infection days later.

Picture the deer as a soup can, I tell myself as I lift the gun. I've nailed plenty of those. Lifting the rifle, I push the gun butt into my right shoulder. I position my eye to peer along the sights. I lift the muzzle, aim. My finger curls around the cold trigger.

"Steady," Dad whispers. "Squeeze the trigger. Don't pull it."

My heart pounds like an out-of-control jackhammer.

Soup cans don't have eyes that show innocence and fear. Soup cans don't exhale in fog-gray puffs or have thick necks that hold up crowns of antlers. Soup cans are not beautiful young animals full of life.

"You're taking too long," Dad snaps, straining to keep his voice low. "Shoot!"

I shift. My feet rustle leaves. The buck jumps, snorts a warning to his girlfriends. He stamps a hoof, wheels around. His white-flag tail lifts straight up. He bolts and leaps the way panicked deer do. My trigger finger goes limp. The doe scatter into the shadows.

"What was that?" Dad spits chewed jelly beans. "You had the perfect opportunity! Why didn't you shoot?" The bear charges out of its cave. "Have I taught you nothing?"

His questions are sucker punches delivered with brass knuckles. I let the gun barrel point at the ground and move the hammer forward, guaranteeing that Granddad's gun won't go off.

"You let an easy shot go!" My father's palm slaps his forehead as if he needs to cram this fact into his brain before he can believe it. "What's wrong with you?"

Good question. What *is* wrong with me? "I'm, I'm sorry." I stare at Dad's boots, certain now that they really are too big for me.

"You're sorry? SORRY?" His eyes bulge. His face resembles an overripe tomato.

I jerk as if he's flung a fistful of his jelly beans at my head. Okay, I didn't shoot a deer, but I didn't kill anyone, either.

He turns his back to me and stomps off. Dried bramble, thin tree limbs, brush, and leaves rip and tear and shatter as Dad storms away from what I've done. Or, what I haven't done.

CHAPTER 3

THE EVENING AFTER

Snap! The third pencil point in less than five minutes bites the dust. A tiny explosion of gray smudges the drool overflowing from the square jaw of my cartoon-style, overmuscled hunter. And I'd just finished cleaning up where the last busted point had slid across his rocket-launching bazooka. "Great." I throw the dead pencil down beside the sofa and pick up a pencil with a fresh point. My other hand grabs my kneadable eraser.

"Joey? What's going on with you?" Philly steps in front of the sofa, pops out her earbuds, and stares hard at me. Her hair, which she calls strawberry blond, is pulled up into a chipmunk's tail at the top of her head. Her scrunched, plucked brows make me wonder, again, why girls yank hairs out of their faces.

How often do I have to give her the same death glare that says *butt out*? I grab the remote from under my thigh, aim it right at her, and thumb-punch the volume button. The roar of the hockey crowd swells.

"You're as stubborn and as uncommunicative as our father." She lifts her pointy chin, looking like a gangly-legged, long-necked bird ready to peck my eyes out. "Why has Dad been out in the garage since you two macho men returned home from the great and mighty hunt?"

I shrug. "He's probably cleaning the guns." Wiping them down, pushing rods tipped with scraps of flannel soaked in solvents down their barrels, oiling the metal, and polishing the wood stocks. Since Mom started traveling, if he's not with his guns in the garage, he's out there fixing some broken lamp, piece of furniture, or knickknack that she'd picked up.

"Cleaning guns for two plus hours? Not unless he's buffing and polishing the weapons of the entire United States Army." Her eyes narrow in on me. "What happened today?"

A soft knock on the back door echoes through the kitchen. Save! Until Phil shoots me a glare that says *I'm not done with you,* before she pivots toward the kitchen.

"Hi, Philly! Oh, you're wearing the necklace that I made for you." Mrs. Davies, our next-door neighbor, claps. "Those blue-gray beads are perfect—the exact color of your eyes."

I crack a smile and straighten from my sofa slump. A visit from Mrs. D might as well be a visit from a favorite grandmother. Philly and I are, she tells us, the grandchildren that she never had. For some reason, she and Mr. D, married forty-one years (and still counting, she insists), never had children.

But Mrs. D visiting tonight is bad timing. What if she bumps into Dad? What if he says something about me hunting today?

Just thinking about this makes me want to cram myself under the sofa. Once I overheard Mrs. D, who is a big-time animal lover (like me and Dad, but different), ask Mom how Dad could be crazy devoted to Claude, but shoot rabbits and deer. *How could Joe's affection and respect for animals include shooting some of them?* Mom explained how deer have no natural enemies anymore, how there'd be too many of them without hunters. They would starve when ice and snow cover what's left of the vegetation. More of them would be hit by cars and trucks, maimed and wounded only to die of infection. Mrs. D about broke out in hives.

"I hope I'm not interrupting." Heavy paper bags crinkle. Mrs. D's silver bangle bracelets tinkle, making the same chaotic music as the wind chimes behind her house.

"You never interrupt," Philly replies, morphing back from fire-breathing dragon sister to normal human being.

"That's what I like to hear," Mrs. D almost sings. "I wanted to drop off a couple things that I picked up while shopping for a neighbor." Containers double thump onto the kitchen table.

"Orange juice! We've been out of that for days." Philly says this as if she's been barely surviving without it. "More granola! And that energy juice that I love." My sister almost purrs. "Mrs. Davies, you're the best. Thank you."

I scrunch up my face, grossed out as I picture that green slime that Philly drinks. Made with (gag) spinach and something called wheat grass. And that granola cereal has more nuts and grains than gerbil food.

"No need to thank me, sweetie," Mrs. D tells my sister. "It's hard for your dad to keep up with everything while your mom's away. Besides, I wanted to stop by to show Joey something."

More paper crinkles, but it's not the thick rustle of grocery bags. I crawl to the left side of the sofa and peer over the back of it, into the kitchen. Mrs. D, short and round, kind of like the cinnamon raisin buns that she loves, is pulling a folded page from the pocket of her husband's barn coat, a thing that is a tent on her.

"Great," Phil says. "You could be what he needs tonight. He's in the living room."

I vault the sofa. "Hey, Mrs. D."

"Joey!" Both of her arms fly up. Her long gray-black hair falls out of its loose knot at the back of her head. "How are you, honey?"

I aim a glare at Phil, warning her not to blurt out an answer.

"Look at this." She unfolds the page. "The Franklin Gallery Art Show in Philadelphia! It gave me this fantastic idea: *You* should enter one of your drawings in this show, Joey!"

Phil sputters, almost busts out in her cackle-laugh. "Mrs. Davies, Joey's cartoons aren't art gallery material."

I stop breathing, squeeze my eyes closed, and keep my lips ziplocked, hoping Mrs. D doesn't give away how much time I spend seriously sketching, how often I visit her to show her my sketches and get pointers on how to draw better. Lucky for me, the farting rumble of a van in serious need of a new muffler comes down our street.

"The Minivan of Death," I tell Philly. As if she doesn't hear it. As if people in China don't hear it.

I came up with the Minivan of Death after Philly's buddy Jeebs (Timothy Jon Fitzgerald, nicknamed "Jeebs" for reasons he won't discuss) gave me a ride to school about a month ago. I was beyond late and dreading another run-in with Principal Stack, our student-eating, pantsuit-wearing, bird-of-prey principal. "The Stack Attack," my buddy Cheets calls her. Because she has her hawk eyes trained on me these days. She thinks I should be *applying* myself. As if I'm one of Philly's nail polishes. Okay, sure, I've been late to school. And yeah, I've blown off homework. Once, a few weeks ago, while Mom was in Florida, I skipped school to practice my two-foot hockey stop. Whatever.

I climbed aboard Jeebs's dented van before I knew it was a coffin on wheels. Seriously. It shakes at thirty miles per hour. Jeebs (or anyone stupid enough to drive the van) has to slam the brake pedal to the floor to slow the death van to a gradual stop. According to Jeebs, the vacuum assist for the power brakes is shot. And fixing it costs more green than he's got. I told him during that ride to school, as I pulled his paperback books out from under my butt, that I could shoot the van in the radiator and put it out of its misery. He didn't think that was funny. The guy has zero sense of humor when it comes to his "sweet ride" (his words).

"That van belongs to Jeebs," I tell Mrs. D. "A kid with a major crush on Philly. At least that's what Lexi says." Alexandra Louise McClellan, my sister's best friend.

"If you want to live to see high school, you'd better stop listening in on my conversations, Little Brother."

I grin. "Philly only likes him as a friend."

Phil gives me one of her *I'll deal with you later* glares as she yanks the elastic band off of her stubby ponytail and shakes out her hair.

"Will Clifford is hot guy *numero uno*," I continue, making my voice go girly high. "He's a junior with *smoking green eyes and biceps to die for*." I bat my lashes.

"You're dead," Phil growls as the maroon '95 minivan sputter-pops to a halt. Van doors creak open and slam shut. The jingle of Jeebs's keys moves through the dark, coming toward the house. Phil slides over to the door, but waits. She always makes Jeebs knock.

As usual, he drums out his usual two raps, one pause, and a final knock before he presses his big, pillow head to the left, middle pane of the window in the door. The print of his nose still marks the same glass square from the last time he showed up here.

When he spots Philly, his grin stretches wide. "There's my princess." He yanks the purple knit hat, pulled down to his eyebrows, off of his head. Scrappy brown hair falls over his eyes as he swings his hat hand forward and bows.

"So wrong in so many ways," I mutter.

Even Mrs. D winces at the awkward discomfort of Jeebs trying too hard.

Phil flings a hard double-barrel glare at him through the window glass. Any minute she'll bare her teeth in a snarl. "You know I hate that nickname."

Of course he knows.

"Let us in, Your Majesty." The van keys clatter as he twirls them around his index finger.

Lexi steps up behind doofus boy and punches his arm. That's why I call her the Cherry Bomb. She is petite, cute, and explosive. Her parents should stick a HANDLE WITH CARE warning onto her forehead.

The second Philly pulls open the door, Lex leaps inside, cutting off stocky and slouching Jeebs in the oversize, gray hooded sweatshirt that he wears almost always.

"Hey, Lex," I say, shooting her my most charming grin.

"Hey, handsome," she says back. Because this is our routine. And then she turns to Philly. "It's Saturday night, girl! Time to play!" Lexi, all shimmering green eyes and openmouthed smile, flicks the ends of her long pink scarf to the beat of her be-bopping feet. According to my sister, if Lex isn't running, she's knitting or dancing.

Jeebs starts humming "Love the One You're With," a sixties tune that he's always singing around Philly.

She spreads her arms wide and push-herds her friends back outside, letting the back door swing closed behind her. Never mind that she's only wearing her black-and-orange Riegelsville High sweats and that the air is colder than a polar bear's butt cheeks, my sister would rather turn into a Popsicle than have her friends catch a whiff of the food-stained dishes soaking in the swamp water of our kitchen sink. She'd die from embarrassment if Jeebs and Lex caught a peek at what's become of Mom's once-organized, clutter-free, bleach-clean house.

"I should go," Mrs. Davies whispers into my hearing aid while reknotting her hair at the back of her head. And then her soft hand pats my arm. This fills me with the kind of warm comfort that comes from Mom's hot chocolate and Dad's crackling fireplace fires.

"Okay, Mrs. D." I yank open the door, probably too quick. Why don't I just announce that I'm glad she's leaving before meeting up with Dad?

"About hanging out with you guys tonight—" Philly pulls the zipper tab on her thermal sweat jacket up and back, up and back between her neck and her waist. But she stops when she sees Mrs. D. "Jeebs, Lex, I'd like you to meet our neighbor, Mrs. Davies."

"*Joanne* Davies?" Jeebs stops jingling his keys. "The artist?"

"One of many," Mrs. D says with a gentle chuckle.

"Wow, nice to meet you. Your paintings sell for serious change," Jeebs says as if Mrs. D doesn't know this. "I read that people pay more for a Joanne Davies painting than most human beings spend on a car."

"It's hard to imagine, I know." Mrs. D, probably blushing, watches her feet as she moves down the cement steps. "Nice to have met you, Jeebs and Lex. Philly and Joey, I'll see you later." Without waiting for a response, she shuffle-jogs out of the puddle of light that comes from the bare bulb over our back door. The scuff of her boots fades after she crosses our driveway.

Our *empty* driveway.

"About hanging out tonight," Phil continues, tucking a stray chin-length piece of her hair behind her left ear as she refocuses on Lex and Jeebs. "Not going to happen."

Jeebs loses his goofy grin. "What? Ahhh, man. That's a bummer. What's the problem?"

"Phil—" I try to keep the worry out of my question. "Where's Dad's truck?"

"I'm guessing that he went grocery shopping." She looks back at her friends. "Which means he will be in a rotten mood when he gets home. Which means I can't go out tonight."

I stare at the short, rutted dirt-and-gravel strip that is our driveway. Dad would rather have a cavity drilled than go shopping for anything, especially on a Saturday night. He should be laid out on the sofa with the channel changer on his chest, watching a fishing or wildlife program.

"Excuse me, Joey? Privacy, please?" Phil throws a thumb at the door, as subtle as a wrecking ball.

Back inside, I make a show of heading for the living room. But I U-turn and drop into a crouch under the window in the kitchen door. I press my good ear against it and turn up the volume on my hearing aid.

"Phil," Lex says. "Your dad is never in a bad mood."

"*Never* is a stretch lately," Philly says. "At least since my mom started traveling."

I nod, picturing Mom's employers, the seventy-plus, short and fragile Zuckermans. Ralph, who calls himself R. Z. and always wears a plaid jacket with a calculator in the side pocket, is, Mom says, a guy who lives to bargain but can never get a person's name right. He calls her Julia or June. Her name is Jill. His wife, Zinnia, dyes her hair the color of a ripe pumpkin, smells of boiled potatoes, and loves to shop for antiques.

"I remember when your mom started working," Lex chimes in. "She was thrilled."

"Two seconds after Joey turned twelve, at the end of my

freshman year. The exact age when she and my dad met. When he was a track star at Riegelsville High," Philly says over the *zip-zip, zip-zip* of her zipper ripping up and down her sweatshirt. "Coincidence? I think not."

I'm not sure what the time and place of when Mom and Dad met have to do with Mom's job, but of course Philly makes this into a soap opera.

"My mom loves the Zuckermans' antique store," Jeebs comments.

Phil sighs. "It would be nice if those Zuckermans could stock it themselves without taking my mom away on so many shopping trips here, there, and every-freakin'-where." My sister taps her foot. "Apparently my mom has always wanted to travel. Who knew?"

"Your mom is finding herself," Jeebs says in this sappy, sensitive-guy voice.

Finding herself? Who said she was lost?

"Antique shopping in Australia during September, more shopping in Florida in October, with two more weeks somewhere else after that. Now she's in Africa. Something about masks and statues." Phil sighs. "Maybe you're right, Jeebs."

Joey, can you imagine being paid to visit places such as Africa? Mom asked me before she left. When I didn't say anything, since Africa pretty much never crosses my mind, she kept going. *I never realized how exciting traveling could be. And I'm making money while doing it. Talk about killing two birds with one stone.*

Something told me that she was killing more than birds, but I kept quiet.

"It shouldn't be so hard to keep up with your own mother." *Zip, zip, zip.*

Philly is right. Mom's trips have become blurry for everyone except her. Sure, she e-mails and calls, tells us that she misses us *soooo* much. But the conversations get uncomfortable with all the blah-blah-blah of how much fun she is having. Dad's expressions go south.

My taking down a buck would have given him something to brag about to Mom. She'd be sorry to have missed the excitement. Maybe sorry enough to hate being away.

"It's hard." Philly gives up the zipping. "My dad mopes when my mom is gone for more than four days. Even the cat has picked up on this. He's been peeing in my mom's good shoes."

Lex gasps. Jeebs snickers.

"That's awful, Phil," Lex says. "Sad."

"When he gets back, I'm going to make stew for dinner," Philly says. "He loves stew."

Correction: Dad loves *Mom's* stew—fresh carrots, potatoes, cubed venison (deer meat), and gravy. Not Phil's pasty canned vegetables mixed with anything from bacon bits to pepperoni slices and jarred gravy that looks like brown Jell-O. After she heats this mess, she drops in balled slices of white bread. She calls these dumplings. I call them disgusting.

"I love stew," Jeebs says, trying to make "stew" sound sexy.

All at once I understand why Claude coughs up fur balls.

"I don't know what's gotten into my mom," Philly continues. "When she's home, she rants about how Joey, Dad, and me expect her to be the maid, the cook, the laundry lady, and the gardener. She says we take her for granted." My sister sighs. "Apparently that's bad."

What do the crusty pots and slimy dishes piled in the sink say about appreciation? How about the growing piles of laundry that even a skunk wouldn't go near?

"Meanwhile, my dad doesn't want anyone complaining to her about how things are without her here." Philly plucks at the beads of her necklace. "He doesn't want her thinking that he can't keep things going around here without her."

"Does he tell her how much he misses her?" Lex's soft question wavers.

"I don't know." Phil shrugs. "My mom and dad, married since the days of the dinosaurs, operate on the theory that not discussing problems means that they'll disappear. Abracadabra."

"I detect marital trouble," Jeebs mutters.

I detect a need to cram his hat (which Lexi probably knit for him) down his throat. Since when is Jeebs a relationship guru? The kid can't even get Philly to be interested in him.

"I've been thinking that, too," my sister admits.

This puts me on hold.

"Believe me, spending a Saturday night at home is not my idea of a good time, but I can't leave my brother here alone to deal with my dad's mood. Not to mention the groceries."

"One is the loneliest number," Jeebs points out.

I might have to use my life savings to buy him a skirt.

"I don't get any of this," Lex snaps. I picture her throwing her hands up, shaking her head hard enough to make her short black hair and long bangs fly in every direction. "Your parents have always been close. Practically attached at the hip."

That's right. Lex knows. She's been here enough, has had a front-row seat to plenty of Mom and Dad's PDA (parental displays of affection)—hugs, hand-holding, kisses.

"Okay, Phil," Lex says. "Jeebs and I will let you be a homebody tonight."

I lift up onto my knees, slow, until I can peer out the bottom of the window.

Of course the girls are clenched in a good-bye hug. When Lex spin-turns and skips down the steps, Jeebs flings open his orangutan arms and wraps them around my sister as if everyone had been playing Simon Says and Simon called "Hug Philly." She turns to rock, probably not appreciating this Jeebs affection or the way he's humming "Love the One You're With." Again.

That's when Claude saunters out from the backyard darkness and past the BEWARE OF CAT sign that Mom carved and painted in some woodworking class, after the cat, who hates hairy man legs, attacked the calves of a UPS guy wearing shorts.

As Claude climbs the cement steps, slow, he eyes Jeebs with pure suspicion.

"Hey, Claws." Jeebs reaches down to pet the cat.

Big mistake. Claude takes a swing. He misses Jeebs's hand only because he chooses to.

"His name is Claude," Philly reminds Jeebs. "As in 'I'm clawed and dangerous. Keep your distance, human, especially if you're a male.' Be glad that you didn't lose a finger. My dad and Joey are the only guys Claude likes."

Mostly Dad, since he rescued the cat from a shelter.

With his hands raised, like he's being robbed, Jeebs backs down the steps, watching Claude without blinking. "This proves my theory that cats are aliens—superior life-forms here to take over our planet."

Philly shakes her head at her friend. "See you later." Her voice leaks sadness.

I get myself back into the living room and nosedive onto the sofa. I flip open my drawing pad just as the back door hinges creak.

As Philly comes to the sofa, Claude jumps onto the back of it. I lift a pencil like I've been using it for the last twenty minutes. On the television, some ex–pro hockey player turned commentator, a guy with chunky false teeth and a bad rug, bounces in his seat and flings his arms while describing a fight on the ice.

"I thought you were taking off with Jeebs and Lex," I say.

My sister sighs, pushes hair behind her ear. "I have an A.P. bio paper to write."

The A.P. for Advanced Placement. This is Philly: cross-country and track star, A-plus student, perfect daughter. I glance at the table in front of the sofa where the one and only textbook that I brought home for the weekend waits for me, unopened. Okay, yeah, I should have brought more books home. But homework isn't my favorite thing. This is me: C-minus student into a sport my parents don't understand.

"You'd better get some homework done, too," Phil says on her way to her room.

"No way." I stand. "I'm going to watch the rest of this game with Jacks, Katz, and Cheets." The hockey posse: Jacks, the right wing for our team, Katz, our awesome defenseman, and Cheets (real name Tony Cheetavera), our goalie. "Junior, too," I add. If Junior (real name Chuck Hector) can leave his house. If his dad, Sam, goes to the Hunter's Inn for the night, which he's been doing a lot the last few months.

"I'm out of here," I add. Away from everything hunting. To Jacks's house, to hang out with the guys who know me best. I grab the remote and flick off the hockey game, but then the rumble of Dad's Jeep slides up our driveway.

I whip around to face the back door for the first glimpse of Dad's mood. Claude dives off the sofa and flies into the kitchen.

Zip, zip, zip goes Philly's zipper. "Don't worry," she whispers in this weird, comforting tone. Since Mom's first business trip, Philly occasionally morphs into our mother.

"Don't worry?" I turn, giving her a squinty expression that asks if she's from Mars. "Phil, Dad's mood is my fault."

One of her eyebrows arch. "Joey, whatever happened in the woods today is the least of his problems."

I'm about to inform her that she doesn't know what she's talking about when the kitchen door slams open. Plastic bags rustle. Heavy things land with thuds on the kitchen table. Groceries.

"Anyone home?"

"In here, Dad," Philly calls in a too-sweet-to-be-true voice.

"Okay." The kitchen door opens and slams shut again.

I shove my sketch pad under a sofa cushion.

Phil twists her face at me. "What are you doing?"

"I don't want him to see that I've been drawing." Or hear him say, again, with about as much respect as he gives his jelly beans, *Art is a nice hobby, son, but what good can come of it?* The same question he's asked about hockey.

That's my dad—practical, sensible. Hunting rates high with him because it teaches responsibility and respect for nature. It builds character, provides food.

"Please, Joey. He doesn't care about your cartoons or comic strips." My sister flicks her hand as if batting the idea aside. "What'd you do today that's so terrible? Did you kill someone? Did Dad catch you burying the body under a porch?"

"An M. K. Buckner dig. How original, Phil. You're about as funny as the flu." I glance at the back door again. "I let a deer go. Okay? A buck. I had a clear shot at him, but I couldn't pull the trigger." I wait for her to say that she's glad that I didn't shoot an innocent animal.

"That's it?" She sighs. "Joey, Dad's mood has nothing to do with that." She plants her hands on her bony hips. "You froze when it came time to shoot a deer. You got buck fever."

I stiffen. Buck fever is nothing to be proud of. Not among hunters.

"Face it, brother of mine, you're not a hunter."

"Don't say that," I growl through clenched teeth.

"Remember how upset you got when Chester, the rabbit, died? And let's not forget that time when we watched *Bambi*. You were a mess."

"Shut up, Phil." Really, I might strangle her.

"Joey, you're not Dad. Don't try to be."

"He needs me to be a hunter. He needs me to be his

hunting buddy. The way he was for Granddad. The way the MacTagerts have always been." Especially now that Mom isn't around.

More rustling comes through the kitchen doorway, along with Dad's grumbling.

I snatch my drawing pad from under the cushion. I yank out my hearing aid and almost sprint across the living room to my bedroom. I pull the door closed behind me, as if this is all I need to do to escape this day.

CHAPTER 4

SUNDAY, THE SECOND DAY

I cruise the empty house as I pop Cheez Doodles, my breakfast, into my mouth. Why not? No one is here to tell me how bad junk food is for me. The odds are good that Dad is at a diner paying for a decent cup of coffee and a grilled pork roll and cheese sandwich. Last Sunday he brought back something with broccoli for Philly and a bacon sandwich for me. But that was before yesterday.

Not long ago, Mom cooked pancakes or waffles every Sunday morning while Dad sat at the kitchen table reading interesting newspaper stories to her. As I stared at television cartoons. And Philly slept. When breakfast was ready, Dad would bang on her bedroom door. He'd click off the television. We'd gather at the kitchen table to eat and talk and laugh.

The reality of how different life has become makes a cheese puff stick in my throat.

As I pass the table in front of the sofa, my textbook whispers *vocabulary sentences* in a tone that sounds too much like Mom's voice. "Later," I tell the book. After hockey.

At the doorway of Philly's room, I pause. Her running journal lies open in the middle of her made bed, below arranged pillows. Two steps into her room and I can make out the page where she logs in her running times, which means that she's off sneaker-pounding pavement. Weird. For a Sunday.

When she comes home from running, she'll scribble her time and how she ran in the journal. She'll note relevant information such as weather conditions. She might even visit the pages where she lists the performance times she wants to beat and the ones she's already buried.

I flip pages until I get to the best part of this journal, which Phil thinks is hidden in the back. The place where she writes her diary entries. I glance back at the doorway, turn up the volume on my hearing aid. If Phil catches me in her room, she'll skin me like I'm a dead rabbit.

My fingers flip the diary pages to Saturday, December 1. Yesterday. My eyes scan Philly's slanted, hard-lined script until I pick out my name: *Joey might be right,* my sister wrote. *Dad probably would be happier if Joey had shot that buck this afternoon. His first day out hunting was a big deal to Dad. I heard him call it a rite of passage. A hunter's bar mitzvah.*

"I knew it," I mumble. After turning the pages back to

the running times, I head for the hunting room, crunching the last cheese puff. Before I'm out of the living room, though, the phone rings. I grab the portable. "Hello." My voice is raspy with powdered cheese.

"Dude, where were you?"

"Hey, Cheets." I start toward the hunting room again.

"You missed an intense game last night. We thought you were coming over to watch it."

"Yeah, I was. But I got stuck here," I say.

Cheets grunts. "Junior didn't show, either. He had to take care of his old man," Cheets says in a lowered voice. "You know."

Not really. None of us know, really.

We understand that Junior's dad considered himself the best hunter around. He told us so. We know how a sharp branch pierced his eyeball. About a year ago. How he lost his "eagle eyesight" (his words) and his reputation went from being the top-dog hunter with all the jokes to the loudmouth drunk. Cheets, who hangs out with Junior more than the rest of us (they shoot at targets together), claims to have seen Sam backhand Junior more than once since the man lost his job and Junior's stepmom left them. In that order.

We also know, thanks to Cheets, that Sam started relying on Junior to help him hunt after the eye injury. They needed the deer and rabbit meat. Other than that, though, the guys don't know much. Junior is tight-lipped about his dad and home life. When he shows up at school with a bruise or a gash, he doesn't talk about it.

Cheets clears his throat. "Anyway, you're going to be at the rink today, right?"

I step into the hunting room, eye the four sets of mounted antlers on the walls. Four of the best racks from the bucks that Dad has brought down. The space that remains, he's told me, is saved for the antlers of my first buck.

"Hello, Tags? Tell me that you are going to be at the rink today."

"Of course," I finally say. "One o'clock, like always."

"Cool," he says with obvious relief.

There is no hunting allowed on the Sundays that fall within deer season, but I want to get in some practice before heading to the rink. A few shots before hockey might help me shake off yesterday. And if Dad comes home to find me shooting at targets, he might feel better, too.

In the garage, I go to Dad's favorite toolbox. Score! One of the keys to the gun closet is still taped to the inside of the lid, right where I'd seen him hide it a few weeks ago.

After I peel the key free, I fly back to the hunting room and insert the key into the lock on the gun closet door. Metal clicks, a bolt retracts. The door swings open. Dad's guns are lined up like soldiers at attention. I grab the .22 caliber rifle and then a box of ammunition from the shelf.

Of course the phone rings before I get a sweatshirt on. Should I pick it up? But I'm running out of time. Don't pick up? But the teapot clock over the back door says eleven forty-five. Mom calls at noon every Sunday while she's away. And she's called early the last two weeks. Missing her call isn't an option. So I lean the .22 against the wall in the hunting room, drop the box of ammo, and go for the phone. "Hello?"

"Hi, my man!" Mom's tone hits high notes that I didn't think possible. "My man" has been her name for me since I turned twelve. "I miss you."

"Hey, Mom!" The image of her at our kitchen table fills my head. I see her sipping tea or coffee with enough cream and sugar to make it the flavor of ice cream. I hear her humming one of her favorite lullabies, something she's done for as long as I can remember. She says lullabies remind her of when Phil and I were babies in her arms.

"How are you? It's great to hear your voice. What's going on? How's school? How's hockey? Have you gone hunting with your dad yet? Is everything okay at home?"

Even though I'm used to Mom's rapid-fire questions, I jerk at each one the way I flinched when Katz whipped M&M's at Jacks and me after we made fun of his new watch. "I'm good," I lie. To make Mom happy, which might, in turn, make Dad happy. Nobody needs a repeat of last Sunday, when Mom's voice turned squeaky after Philly let slip that we'd eaten pizza without any salad for dinner four times in five days. Dad spent the next hour defending pizza to Mom, promising to make some of her salads, and assuring her that she didn't need to worry about us.

"How was your week? What's new? Tell me about everything that I've missed!"

I hold my breath, dreading a repeat of the hunting question. I know it will come. Because Mom has been almost as worked up about me hunting as Dad has been. She calls my becoming old enough to hunt a "milestone."

"Hockey is great," I blurt out, practically screaming into her ear. "We've got a big game coming up in Jersey. Coach wants me to start."

"Joey, that's great!" She's trying to sound excited, but it's hard for her to get worked up about hockey until she sees me on the ice.

And then I get the long pause. Uh-oh.

"I hope that I'm home for that match." Her voice wavers. "R. Z. and Zinnia are talking about another trip."

"Game," I correct her, fidgeting because she sounds as if she's about to cry. So I don't say *You'd better not miss it.* Up until this year, she never missed a game. She wasn't even late, ever. She never skipped Philly's cross-country or track meets, either.

She sucks in a deep breath, which means she's about to change the subject. "Joey, you should see the beautiful African masks and statues that I've been finding here. You can't believe how tricky it is to get them back to the States, but I'm managing it all. R. Z. and Zinnia keep telling me how impressive I am."

It's uncomfortable hearing Mom all proud of herself. Still, I force a cheesy grin, as if she can see me.

"I've been very busy, have hardly had time to think."

When she giggles, I force a lame chuckle to go along with her.

"I wish you could see the markets here, Joey. They are incredible. Not anything you've ever seen before and—"

The kitchen door bangs open. Philly busts into the room as the hands of the teapot clock come together at the twelve. I stretch my neck to see past her. Where's Dad?

"Is that Mom?" Phil comes at me, red faced and sweaty, her hair in a stubby chipmunk's tail on top of her head. After she yanks out her earbuds, which are buzzing with an alternative rock tune, one of her hands, open and outstretched, reaches for the phone. Her fingers curl in, clawing at air, demanding. If Jeebs saw his princess now, he'd lose some of his Philly love.

"Gotta go, Mom. Phil's gonna wet herself if she doesn't talk to you in the next two seconds." I shoot my sister a glare to let her know that under normal circumstances I would not be giving up the phone this easy. But I'll do anything to avoid talking to Mom about hunting.

"Okay, my man," she says. "Look up at the stars and think of me looking at them, too," she adds instead of saying good-bye, the way she's been doing since she's been traveling.

As I start to pass the phone to Phil, Mom's voice, distant and watery through the plastic, calls, *I love and miss you, Joey.*

I want to ask her if she loves and misses Dad, too. Instead I move my mouth closer to the phone. "Miss you, too," I say before my sister grabs hold of the portable.

"Hi, Mom!" Phil busts into a huge grin as she presses the phone to her head. "I'm fine, except that it rots being the lone female in a house full of maleness and testosterone."

Phil bends over the counter, leans her forearms onto it, holding the telephone to her ear with her shoulder, and then launches into a dramatic recap of her life. When she unscrews one of her nail polish bottles and starts painting her fingertips, I return to the hunting room and grab the rifle and the ammo. While my sister blabbity-blabs to Mom, I pad across the kitchen and out the back door without her noticing. Score!

Since I've got negative time to set up (Dad should already be here to talk to Mom), I bolt back into the garage. I grab two blond Barbies and one brunette from the boxes of toys that Mom keeps saying she is going to donate to charity. If she can ever bring herself to get rid of Philly's old dolls and stuffed animals or my trucks and army figures.

Once I get to the backyard, I set down the unloaded .22 and rush over to the sections of fence that separate our lawn from the scrappy lot with the hills of bulldozed dirt and rock left over from what would have been a development of houses, if the builder hadn't gone bankrupt. The perfect target-shooting backdrop. I make the blond doll, with the chopped chunks of what looks to be beaver-chewed hair, straddle the fence. Beside this victim of Philly's first pair of scissors, I position the other two Barbies.

With my back to the house, I load the .22 and lift it to my shoulder. I breathe in cold air. "Time for 'Rambo-Joey Meets the Barbies,'" I mutter, enjoying this. Adrenaline pumps through me as I pull the lever under the rifle down, feel the vibrations of the cartridge clicking into the barrel. My heart shifts into a high gear as I aim, steady and calm. My finger squeezes the trigger nice and slow. *POP!* Barbie with the chewed hair flies up and off the fence in a backflip. I'm pretty sure I nailed her in her ham. Nice shot. Rambo one, Barbies zip.

I am one immense grin until something rustles the high grasses behind the fence. My adrenaline turns to wet cement. My stomach sinks to the soles of my feet.

Oh, no, no, NO!

Winston, Mrs. D's rust-brown, floppy-eared and droopy-eyed old hound, emerges from the grasses on the far side of the fence, moving quick for a dog that lost his left back leg to a hunter's trap. Before he got dumped at a pound, probably because he could no longer hunt.

I stop breathing. My eyes sting from not blinking against

the cold. *Did my Barbie bullet pierce Winston? No, please! Not Winston!*

"Here, boy!" My yell teeters on the edge of panic. Deaf as a stone from years of guns being fired off all around him, the dog keeps running.

With trembling, frantic hands, I unload the .22. All I can think about is how I've got to find Winston.

Always know your target and beyond, Dad's voice reminds me. But I only knew the Barbie.

As if this isn't enough to deal with, a window opens with a metal scrape. "JOEY! What are you doing?"

I don't have to glance over my shoulder to see my sister's pinched frown framed by the window. "Knitting, Phil. I'm out here knitting."

"Are those my Barbies?"

"They're not mine." I drop the unloaded gun close to the house and kick the box of ammunition over to the rifle.

"Tommy Jackson just called. He—"

I take off after Winston.

"Hi, Joey." Mrs. D pauses in the middle of her front lawn, mid–tai chi move. Holding a pose, one leg bent in an upside-down L in front of her, she waves at me. Tai chi, she explained to me once, is a series of slow-motion moves that are a mix of yoga and meditation. Whatever that means. To me, she looks like she can't decide whether to kick someone's butt or dance.

Since she had to have heard the crack of the .22, she must be itching to kick my butt. Sure, she knows that I shoot at crap behind our house. But it doesn't make her happy. Mrs. D and I have reached an understanding. She doesn't ask about why I shoot or whether I'll hunt and I don't tell.

Of course that was before I might have put one of my bullets into her dog.

"Hey, Mrs. D." I force a hand-flip hello up at her. Can she see my fingers trembling?

She glances at Mr. D's watch, a big chunk of silver on her small wrist. "Have you come over to use the studio, maybe work on one of your drawings for the art show?" Her eyebrows arch over an expression beaming hope. Still, her hazel eyes hint of disapproval that mixes with disappointment. A reaction, I'm certain, to the gunshot.

I scan her landscaped yard where bird feeders hang off tree branches like earrings. Where is Winston? I glance over my shoulder at the scrappy pines that border our small yard and the empty driveway. Where is Dad? Why isn't he home to talk with Mom? "Um," I manage to get out, turning back to Mrs. D. "I'm looking for Winston."

"Oh, he's around here somewhere," she says. "Sniffing about."

Or bleeding to death or cowering under a bush, licking at a raw hole that I'm responsible for. I want to curl into a ball and pull my hearing aid out of my ear, to make this go away.

"Your easel is set up and ready for you," Mrs. D adds.

"I can't today." I try to come across as sorry.

"Okay. But you should have a bite of something." She drops her pose, jogs across her front lawn to the brick front steps of her house, and grabs the silver travel mug with the fluorescent-lime print that commands GET GREEN! PLUCKEY'S HERBAL REMEDIES. As she jogs back to me, tea that smells of mint splashes onto the sweatshirt that is huge on her, which means it belonged to her husband. It doesn't matter to her that she is about my height and that Mr. D was an easy six feet tall and twice her weight, she still wears his clothes. Mr. D, who died a year ago, called her his "chickadee" because she is as cute as those little birds that flit about the feeders.

"I picked up roast beef and onion rolls at the store this morning."

I smile. Mrs. D is 100 percent vegetarian, but knows roast beef is one of my favorite foods. She'd chew on her front lawn before she'd chow down on cow, but she'd never hesitate to make me a meat sandwich.

Without waiting for me to answer, she dashes for the garage, waving one arm in scoops that beckon for me to follow her.

As I do, I search for Winston with growing desperation. The reality of what I might have done sinks deeper into me with each step. Knowing that I can't undo this is turning me inside out.

"There's my pup," Mrs. D chirps from inside the garage.

I stop, waiting for the horror. The shriek doesn't come. I take a step forward. And then another step. Still nothing. At a box turtle's pace I move into Mrs. D's shadowy garage.

Thumpity, thump, thump. Winston's thick tail beats an almost musical rhythm on the rungs of the banister along the three steps leading up to the house and door. He pants openmouthed and as smiley as a dog with mud-flap jowls can get.

Mrs. D strokes his head and then opens the door for him. He leaps inside as quick as any dog with four legs. As quick as any dog that hasn't been shot.

Breathing sweet relief, I follow Mrs. D into the redbrick kitchen with brass pans and molds hanging on the walls. The aroma of warm cinnamon, baked apples, and sugar mix with the vanilla cream scent of Mrs. D's burning candles. Easy-listening music plays in the background, as usual. Instead of explaining that I've got to get to the hockey rink, I follow the dog, needing to be sure that he hasn't been grazed by my bullet, isn't bleeding from some unseen wound.

Mrs. D pulls off her tai chi slippers and drops them by the door. Then she slides over to the oven in loose, wool socks big enough to have belonged to Mr. D. She spills more tea.

"Mrs. D—" I blink at the two pies on the stovetop. "You baked?" This question has a *no way* tone to it. Everyone who knows Mrs. D understands that she only uses her oven to warm food bought at the health food store. Mr. D was the cook.

"Believe it or not, I've been baking a pie now and again for the last couple months." She turns to the stove, pushes one of the pies to the back of it. "You know that I don't love to bake, but it is not unpleasant when I'm doing it for someone else."

"Yeah, I get that," I say. And I wonder if shooting a deer might not be so bad if I could remember that I'm doing it for Dad.

"Today I attempted two pies since you love apples. Try a piece, Joey." She pulls a spatula from a drawer. "Tell me if it's any good."

The hands on the wall clock painted with ivy vines that mirror the stuff growing in the ceramic pots arranged all over her kitchen and sunroom point to 12:40. Only twenty minutes until I'm supposed to be on the ice with the guys. I scan the kitchen for Winston.

"Tell me, what are you drawing these days? What are you working on?"

Not much, I don't say. *I've been too busy shooting at targets.*

As Mrs. D pulls open a cabinet and slides out a plate, I spot Winston on the floor, under the kitchen table, muttering to himself. I head over to my usual seat. "By the way, Mrs. D, I still have your camera. I haven't forgotten about it. Really." Sure, avoiding her question is obvious and lame, but I can't tell her about what I've been doing.

"I'll make you a deal, Joey." She glances over her shoulder, gives me her ultra-big grin. It makes her eyes shine.

It also means that she's trying to nudge me into something. Mrs. D has a history of persuading people to do what she thinks is best for them. According to Philly, Mrs. D introduced Mom to the Zuckermans after Mom complained about her "babies" no longer needing her.

Sometimes I wonder if Mrs. D knows how much trouble that move started.

She also persuaded Philly and Lexi to eat and drink green and grainy health foods. Stuff made from dandelions, grasses, and leafy things meant for sheep and goats.

"Studying photos of animals can help you to draw them," Mrs. D continues. "If you promise me that you'll keep taking pictures of animals and using the photos to draw, then you can keep the camera for as long as you'd like."

Not sure if I can make this promise, I drop to my knees beside the dog and run my hands over him, mostly petting him but also checking for any injuries, just to be sure he's okay. "Thanks, but if I don't get that camera back to you soon, you might never see it again. I'm the best at losing stuff."

Mrs. D starts carving a wedge of pie big enough to feed a troop of Boy Scouts. "Have you thought at all about entering that art show in Philadelphia?"

Winston flops onto his back, all three feet in the air, his

tongue hanging out one side of his mouth. Overflowing with gratitude, I rub his bullet-free belly.

Mrs. D's voice remains chirpy. "The Franklin Gallery Art Show would be the perfect opportunity for you to exhibit a drawing. It would be great exposure."

I start to itch—an allergic reaction to exposure.

If Mrs. D had her way, she'd paste my drawings on one of those huge billboards along Interstate 95.

The long hand on the ivy clock ticks off another minute. Only ten left until I should be in skates.

"This art show is a kind of contest, Joey. The judges will comment on your work and compare it with the other drawings in the show." She glances over her shoulder again. "I know you enjoy competition."

Sure. When it comes to hockey. But I'm not loving the image of stuffy judges pointing and snort-laughing at one of my drawings until their dentures pop out and hit the floor. I'm trying to avoid picturing Mom's face pinched with concern and weighed down with disappointment because my schoolwork isn't a priority. Or Dad's face broadcasting hurt as it dawns on him that I'd rather be drawing and entering art contests than hunting with him. *Not bad, son,* he had said a few weeks back when he caught me sketching a deer. After I told him the piece was just an art project, he applied an affectionate shoulder slap. *It won't be long before you get your hunting license and can start shooting deer instead of drawing them.* And then he grinned big. As if we understand each other and share a burning desire to hunt. As if this means everything to him.

Mrs. D slides the pie slab onto a plate. "Anyway, Joey, I'd like to sponsor you."

"Sponsor me?" This sounds dangerous. I am starting to wonder if the pie is a bribe.

"I'll get your drawing matted and framed. I'll take care of all the fees and paperwork." Mrs. D takes a fork from a drawer, balances it on the plate, and walks it over to me. "All you need to do is pick out the drawing that you like best and give it to me to enter into the show." She pushes aside a bowl filled with chopped carrots, whole apples, and celery sticks—lunch for the rabbits and deer in her backyard. For the squirrels, there will be corn chips and nuts.

The fork clinks as she places the plate of pie on the table in front of me. My stomach gurgles but my head screams that I need to return the .22 to the gun closet before I haul my tail in double time to the hockey rink.

"Thanks, Mrs. D." I'm talking about the pie, not the sponsor offer. I start shoveling apples and pastry into my mouth in a way that would horrify Mom. Now that I know I didn't shoot old Winston, I'm starved. Cheese puffs don't hold up under stress.

"How about that roast beef sandwich, Joey?"

This pie and the sandwich could be my only decent meal of the day. On Sunday nights Phil makes waffles that are harder than Wiffle balls or hamburgers that make hockey pucks seem edible. I actually miss Mom's salads. But I can't stick around here any longer than it takes me to inhale this apple pie. Still, I can't say no—my mouth is too full.

So, of course, Mrs. D goes to the refrigerator and pulls out the clear plastic deli packet of sliced roast beef. "Entering the art show would be a fine first step in getting your talent out into the world where people can see it, Joey."

Where people can see it. I almost gag.

"This kind of recognition can lead to art school scholarships. So, think about my offer, okay, Joey?"

Swallowing wet paper towel would be easier than my mouthful. "Okay," I finally get out. But *okay* really means "I'll think about the offer." And that's it.

"Good." She lays out six bread slices and distributes meat to three of them. "Would it be too pushy of me to ask you to come over after hockey practice tomorrow to show me what you've been working on?"

Another hunk of pie hangs by fork in front of my mouth. "You know I love coming over here, Mrs. D." Not just for the art lessons, either. Not just for my own easel. Not just for the charcoal pencils, the kneaded erasers, or the other five million cool art things that Mrs. D gives to me. I come over because she is fun to hang out with. And, she knows more about drawing than my art teacher, Mr. Leo. Plus, she always has bakery cookies.

"I'll get back here as soon as I can," I tell her.

"Fantastic." She wraps the three sandwiches in aluminum foil and then glances up at the wall clock. I could have told her that it's one o'clock. And that I'm late.

"Keep eating, Joey. Don't mind me." After she drops the foil-wrapped sandwiches into a brown paper bag, she goes to the drawer where she keeps scissors, tiny pliers, and string. She pulls out a bead choker and places it near the uncut pie. "I just have something that I need to do."

"Something I need to do" has a mysterious edge to it, but I've got no time to dwell on this.

"Actually, Mrs. D, I've got to go." The chair feet scrape against the tile floor. Winston mumbles what might be doggie disappointment as I jump up.

"Okay, Joey." She hurries over to me with the bag of sandwiches. "For you, your sister, and your dad."

"Thanks." And I mean it. Philly says Dad gets uncomfortable taking everything that Mrs. D passes off to us while Mom is gone. Not me. I've got nothing but appreciation.

With a last wave, I head for the door, leaving a hunk of pie on the plate, which is a first for me. I tear into a roast beef sandwich the second I'm in the garage. It's half gone by the time I put away the gun and ammo, return the gun-closet key to the toolbox, and hit our driveway—which is still empty.

CHAPTER 5

MONDAY, THE THIRD DAY

Dragging myself across the shadowy living room isn't easy. I'm pretty sure someone poured cement into my sneakers while I slept. I'm almost to the kitchen when I glance at the master bedroom. Behind its half-opened door, an ivory-comforter-covered lump lies diagonally across the king-size bed, mashing Mom's fringed silk pillows. They are *not* meant for anyone to sleep on. The lacy comforter is not supposed to be drooled on. Stale smoke, which can only be from other people's cigarettes, burns the inside of my nose. Dark jeans and thick white socks on big feet poke out from under the comforter, along with one navy blue flannel-shirted arm. Since when does Dad sleep in his clothes? Why didn't he get up at five a.m. to go for a run?

All of a sudden, sad oozes through me. My steps get heavier as I head for the kitchen again, where the sink stink is mixing with the funk of an old pizza and the tang of an overripe banana. “What’s Dad doing home still?” I jerk my thumb hard toward the master bedroom.

Philly darts across the kitchen with an open bag of ground coffee, already digging a measuring spoon into it. “I told you that I think he’s depressed.” She two-step hops over Claude. Even though she’s wearing her black sweats with the tiger-orange trim, her hair is neat and dry. Her sneakers are laced, but her face isn’t flushed.

When I don’t say anything, she pauses at the coffeemaker, turns to me. “Having Mom gone so much really bites, doesn’t it?”

I look down at my sneakers. “Yeah.” The teapot clock ticks. “It feels worse when he’s—” I glance over my shoulder as if I can see into the master bedroom.

“What about you?” With her right hand, Philly messes up my overgrown hair. “Did you get the license plate number of the truck that ran you over this morning?” She gives me one of her I’m-so-adorable-I-can-hardly-stand-myself grins.

The back of my hand knocks her fingers off of my head. Part of me wants to tell her that I don’t care if my hair is in place and that, by the way, I might not stick around here long enough this morning to find a comb or a brush. Why would I? I sure don’t want to run into Dad.

“Is it mud brown or mud crusted?” Her long fingers tug on a clump of my bangs.

"Cute, Phil, real cute." Again I knock her hand off of me. I could do this all day. "I washed it last night, okay?"

"Were you up all night doing it?" She blinks at me, loses some of her playful. "Seriously, Joey, your eyes are puffy. And your face. Milk has more color." Doing her best Mom impression, she tips her head to observe my left ear as she plants her hands on her hips. Another annoying habit that Phil has picked up since Mom started traveling. "Where's your hearing aid?"

"Where's your search warrant?" It's getting hard to keep my voice low.

Now she squints. Her mouth puckers. Good-bye gentle Philly, hello impatient I-didn't-get-my-morning-run Phil.

Wrestling with a cougar would be less painful than messing with my sister right now. Mom says Philly inherited her constant craving to pound pavement and dirt from Dad. That's why, as much as I hate giving in to her, I reach into the front pocket of my jeans and pull out the plastic, flesh-colored hearing aid. I hold it up with a jerk of my wrist. "Happy?"

Waiting for me to put the stupid thing into my ear, she stares at me without blinking or flinching. I give this right back to her for a good minute (okay, maybe only fifteen seconds). This is a kind of showdown. Claude, who couldn't care less about our standoff, curls around my shins, trying to trip me. This is the thanks I get for feeding him while Mom is missing in action. When he starts mewing like he's starving to death, I give in and shove the hearing aid into my ear. "You're a jerk," I inform Phil. And then I head for the refrigerator to get the cat's food.

"You're not the only one feeling the tension around here, Little Brother." She points the measuring spoon, dusted in dark grains, at my face. "I've got a hangover spelled e-x-h-a-u-s-t-i-o-n from being up until two a.m., waiting for Dad to drag his carcass home."

"What?" I whip around to face her. "He didn't come home until *two*?"

"Not a minute before. And by the smell of him, I'd say that he was at the Hunter's Inn. Cigarette smoke is a door prize of that joint."

I blink, my mouth hanging open. The Hunter's Inn, a dark and narrow old shack with a long and substantial bar, a few wobbly tables with even wobblier chairs, and a couple pinball machines pushed up against wood-paneled walls, under dusty mounted antlers. Neon beer brands glow in the only windows, on either side of the door. I know. Cheets and I went with Junior into this place once to retrieve his father.

But why would Dad hang out in the Hunter's Inn? "He doesn't drink anything stronger than black coffee," I say, as if Philly doesn't know this. His worst vice has always been a tie between his addiction to jelly beans and his love of the greasy pork roll sandwiches that he gets at the New Jersey diners (he says Jersey has the best pork roll). "Going to the Hunter's Inn on a Sunday is not Dad's style."

"Apparently it is now." Philly sighs as she turns back to the coffeemaker.

Is this why Dad blew off Mom's Sunday telephone call? To go to the Hunter's Inn?

"I think he's lonely." Philly flicks the coffeemaker switch hard. The machine gurgles and drools brown. A roasted nut aroma starts to cover the nastier smells hanging in the room.

I roll my eyes at her know-it-all diagnosis. Talking about this feels wrong. Weird.

As I pull open the refrigerator door, Claude starts in with his high-pitched demands of *Feed me NOW!* As much as I adore him, I consider drop-kicking him into the living room.

Philly sidesteps to the sink and yanks open the dishwasher door. Bunching her nose and curling her top lip, she shoves her sleeves up her forearms and plunges her hands into the swamp water. "I'm worried. Dad never skips his morning jog. He's like me. Running invigorates him. Think about it: Even his bad leg has never stopped him." She sighs. "Everything is wrong. Look at me—skipping my morning run to make coffee to get Dad to work before noon." She crams a handful of spoons and forks into the dishwasher basket. They scrape and *ting*. "And loading dishes that *you* were supposed to deal with."

Will the clink of dishes wake Dad up? I shoot a quick glance into the living room.

"By the time I'm done, I'll have no time left to study this morning." Phil shakes her head. "This bites. I wanted to get a jump on conjugating a few Spanish verbs."

Spanish is her favorite subject. *Mi tema preferido,* she says.

Claude jumps onto the counter, which he is not allowed on, and head-butts my shoulder. Any minute he'll start swiping at me, so I turn back to the refrigerator. I grab the gallon of milk and the container of orange juice that Mrs. D brought over. They hit the kitchen table with dual *thunk*s. Next, I fling a squat cat food can. The smiling cat face on the orange plastic top that covers the can (something only Mom would buy) spins into the milk carton. After that, I Frisbee-throw a foil-wrapped triangle, a left-over slice of pepperoni pizza. It lands with a *splat* onto the table. Claude flings himself off the counter like he's a flying squirrel.

"Things don't seem right between Mom and Dad," Philly mutters as if she's sharing top secret information. Now that the dishes are stowed and the stink water is being sucked down the drain, she pours herself a bowl of the health-food cereal that Mrs. D brought over.

I shake my head. "Why can't Mom and Dad just be the way that they've always been?"

"Good question." Philly brings her bowl to the table, hopping around Claude, who is four-paw rumba dancing, as I dump Seafood Supreme, which smells of low tide, into the special bowl with "Claude" hand-painted on it by Mom. Only she would worry that someone might confuse the cat's dish with one of her salad plates.

As Philly grabs the milk container and pours white over the cereal, I rip foil and cram cold pizza into my face.

Philly stares at me over floating granola. Her teeth grind a spoonful of it, a sound like a blender tearing apart bark. "I think Mom is trying to find herself," she says after swallowing.

"That's your idiot friend Jeebs talking." I almost spit pepperoni into her cereal.

"I think Jeebs is right, Joey."

"That's frightening." Not to mention annoying.

"She and Dad got married young." Philly jabs the spoon into her cereal. "Maybe, now that we're older, she wants to do things she didn't do before getting hitched and having kids. Like traveling."

I gulp-swallow. Philly stares into her cereal. Only Claude, who is practically licking the paint off of his bowl, shows any enthusiasm for his food.

Phil's attention shifts to the spot by the back door where my hockey pads lay beside my skates. "Where's Flyer? Don't tell me you forgot your precious hockey stick."

Flyer, named after the Philadelphia Flyers. The greatest hockey team ever.

"That stick's usually attached to you like a fifth limb." Phil's eyes narrow in on my face.

Even though my hunger has shrunk to nothing, I inhale more pizza. "Forget it."

The coffeemaker burbles that it has finished brewing. Phil doesn't care. She leans forward, points her spoon at the space between my eyes. "There isn't going to be any hunting this afternoon. Dad can't take the time off during the week."

No kidding. Besides, how could I hunt when I'm still spooked at having almost shot Winston? I grab the orange juice container and tip it to my mouth, ignoring Phil's laser glare.

"You're too gross for words." She contorts her face.

"Thank you." Bits of juice-soaked pizza fly out of my mouth.

"Listen to me, weasel-boy: Dad's no-hunting-alone rule is NOT to be broken."

"Keep it down." I tilt my head toward the master bedroom.

The spoon jabs again, closer to my nose, flings a drop of milk against my cheek. "If Dad ever catches you hunting without him, you'll be ninety pounds of dead meat."

Not good considering I weigh eighty-five pounds with my sneakers on. "Like I don't know that, Phil," I snap, trying not to crack a whisper.

This gets me another sigh. "Joey, please." Now her voice is cotton soft. "Don't do anything to make life any rockier around here, okay?"

"Butt out, Phil." I spit crumbs. Claude dives for cover. "Don't talk to me about hunting."

Philly places her spoon into her bowl. "Joey, you do know that hunting, shooting a deer, has nothing to do with whatever's going on between Mom and Dad, right?" She stares me down. "You do understand that they have to work things out themselves. Or not." She takes in a deep breath and then lets it out. She doesn't even blink. "Think about the animals, not about making our father happy. Going after innocent, living things with weapons isn't fair."

I almost holler *I THINK ABOUT THEM ALL THE TIME!* Instead, I close my eyes and hope that she doesn't launch into an animal-rights speech.

"If you ask me, you already do feel for the animals. That's why you couldn't—"

"You don't get it," I say, raising my voice over hers. "Dad and me hunting together is about family tradition. It's about me being a MacTagert and his hunting buddy."

"Sure, sure. Father-son bonding, finding something you two have in common, the importance of you fitting into his boots," Phil adds. "Believe me, I get it." One of her eyebrows arches in a kind of danger signal. "I also get," she says, low and serious, "that if you hunt solo, I'll rat you out to Dad faster than you can say 'I'm grounded for life.' "

My right hand makes a fist, crushes the aluminum foil that had covered the pizza slice.

She stands, takes her bowl and spoon to the sink. "There

are consequences for actions, Little Brother. Remember that. Consequences for breaking Dad's rules." She turns to me, crosses her arms tight in front of her, juts out her right hip, and studies me for a minute. "Maybe I'd better—" She pivots, climbs onto the counter beside the stove. Reaching up, she snakes one arm into the cabinet over the burners. Hollow plastic containers fall, crash, and tumble within the space as Phil fishes out a dented coffee can with something metal clanking inside it. A key spills out, bounces across the tile floor.

Phil hops off the counter, snatches this key, and holds it up to me. "The gun closet key." Lifting her chin, she slides it into the pocket of her sweatpants. "Now you can't hunt."

It's tempting to laugh out loud at how slick she thinks she is.

Looking proud of herself, Phil struts over to the coffeemaker and pours steaming black into the World's Best Dad mug. Next, she grabs the topless aspirin bottle.

Shaking my head at her, I go into the living room and pull the book that I brought home for the weekend toward me. This is risky. If Dad wakes up and catches me doing homework, I'll be worse off than dead. It is understood that I'm supposed to follow Mom's house rules, even when she's gone. The one about getting homework done before going to bed is the number one, no-argument, top-priority rule of all. Whatever. If Mom wanted things done her way, she should have stuck around.

Phil pauses in front of the master bedroom. "What do you think you're doing?"

I don't look at her, but I'm sure she's glaring at me.

"You're not doing homework now," she informs me. "You should have done that Saturday or last night."

I keep scanning the page of questions after the section of text I was supposed to read. I should be concentrating on how to answer them, but instead I'm thinking that if Phil put blond streaks in her hair and smeared on watermelon-colored lipstick, she'd be our mother's clone.

And just like Mom would do, Phil marches around to the front of the sofa, faces me, and points a rigid finger at the textbook, making the tablets in the aspirin bottle rattle. "You fall behind in school again and you'll have to redo seventh grade, Joey."

Or at the very least be forced, again, by Mom and Dad to do hard time with tutors. Like last year, when I blew off too much schoolwork to play hockey. And draw.

Since I don't want to deal with this, I aim a hateful glare at my sister. "Your nose doesn't belong in my business, okay?"

She growls, storms back to the master bedroom, muttering something about idiot brothers.

I lift up onto my knees to watch her place the mug of coffee and the aspirins onto the night table at Dad's side of the bed as he snores and sputters. This is a long way off from the Mom and Dad routine of Mom prepping the coffeemaker each night and Dad hitting the on button each morning. After his run, he'd bring two mugs of the fresh brew into the bedroom where he and Mom would sip and chat while he got ready for work.

I lean left, watch Philly go into our parents' closet-size bathroom with its sea-green walls, starfish border, and shell soaps. Old metal squeals as Philly wrenches the ancient wall faucets of the shower to the on position. With a lot of patience and a bit of luck, hot water might find its way through these rattling pipes by the time Dad crams his bulk into the stall. Not too long ago, he thought cold showers were invigorating. These days, when his sleep tank is close to empty, it seems that only steam and caffeine can get him moving.

When Philly returns to the bedside table, she picks up the alarm clock and starts messing with it. Then she jogs back to me. "Pack it up, Little Brother. Put it into gear. Dad's alarm is set to go off in five minutes. Odds are good he won't wake up full of sunshine and cheer."

I slap my book closed. I pull on another sweatshirt and then a third and add on a zip-up from beside the sofa.

By the time I get into the kitchen, Phil's thrown on her white parka with the fake fur trim. She looks me over as she lifts the strap of her gym bag onto her shoulder. She points at the gaping yawn of my backpack. "One book and a bag of barbecued potato chips?"

"Come on, Phil," I mock in my best impression of her

high-pitched voice as I shove past her and the coat hook that holds my dark blue winter jacket from last year.

"Joey, what's with all the sweatshirts and no coat?"

"It doesn't fit anymore. Okay?" I avoid looking at her.

"No, not okay." She glances at my sneakers. "You don't have boots, either?"

"Whatever."

"Great. And Dad's already too overloaded with work to deal with this," Philly says more to herself than me.

Plus, he'd rather wrestle an alligator in a septic tank than deal with crowds in a mall.

"Here's what we'll do," Phil decides. "Lex and I will shop online."

I scrunch my face at her, thinking the nuts in her health food cereal have gone to her head. "Where are you planning to get the funds, Phil?"

She studies the cracked leather and bologna-skin bottoms of her running sneakers for a moment. "I'll ask Dad for a credit card once he's in a better mood."

I groan. "We need our designated shopper back."

"In the meantime, will you be warm enough in those sweatshirts, Joey?"

"Yes." As if warmth is the problem . . . *Once he's in a better mood,* Phil's voice repeats in my ears.

"See ya." I take off down the steps before she gets to the door. I cut left and slip into the garage. Of course I'm late, again, but at least Philly won't be the only one with a key.

CHAPTER 6

FIVE DAYS UNTIL SATURDAY

"I've gotta go." I slam my locker closed. "I've got to write vocabulary sentences before third-period English with Greasy Greason," I tell Jacks. "Hey, can you give me a sentence using 'shrew'?"

"Sorry, Tags." Jacks grins as we bob and weave through the crowded hallway. His new braces throw off a glare, but I don't give him a hard time. I cut him a break. He's funny about this new metal. When he remembers that he's self-conscious about it, he tries to keep his mouth closed. Believe me, this isn't easy for him.

"I could have written those vocab sentences this morning, if my spastic sister hadn't rushed me out of the house." I stuff the last barbecued potato chip into my mouth and crunch.

Jacks perks up, more alert now. "Philly?" Pink pushes

into his cheeks, clashing with his freckles and cantaloupe-colored hair and announcing his crush.

"Yeah, you've met her one or two billion times." Since I can't remember the Heimlich maneuver, I apply sarcasm. Then I ball up the chip bag and pitch it at his head before cutting left, into the social studies cave. My first class.

Reality smacks me hard as I drop into my seat. Me, the first one at a desk. It's wrong. And for what? To scratch out vocab sentences? This bites.

After a few minutes, Karen LaCross steps through the doorway with her chin lifted, as usual. "Joey?" she squeals. "What are you doing here before the bell?" Her eyebrows arch up under her mud-brown, flat-edged bangs. Her eyes register shock. This is more than annoying.

As she approaches, I slide my forearms over my drawing of hockey players skating around vocabulary words. If Karen the Kiss Up, a girl who always has her hand in the air and thinks she knows everything, figures out that I haven't done my homework, she'll rat me out in less than thirty seconds. Guaranteed.

On the other hand, I'm desperate. "Hey, Kar." I try to sound casual. I lean against the plastic seat back. I roll my pencil between my palms. My I'm-too-cool-for-school attitude. "What sentence did you write for 'motive'?"

"Joey, you are hilarious." Her high-pitched shriek-laugh could drive dogs and people with hearing aids insane. "We're in social studies, not language arts." Shaking her head as if I'm a complete flake, she moves to her desk, which is smack in the middle of the front row.

Why do girls have to be frustrating, stupid, and difficult all at the same time? At the rate I'm going, I'll end up in the library trying to get these sentences written. Yeah, asking our librarian, Ms. Monia, where she keeps the dictionary ought to be a bucket of fun. Encyclopedias have more warmth and sense of humor than that prune-faced woman.

As more of the class flows in, Gina Dembrowski, who talks almost never, slides into the seat next to me. Our teacher, Mr. McNab, put her there on purpose. Something about trying to limit my socializing. Yeah, I've heard this before. *Too much talking* and *too much doodling* are the comments that most of my teachers throw my way, whether I want to hear them or not.

"Hey, Gina." I watch as she aligns three pencils on her desk in a perfect row beside the three textbooks stacked onto two notebooks. "What's up?" I flash my most charming grin. She glances at me from behind a curtain of long and straight yellow hair that smells of fake strawberries. Not even close to smiling, she watches me with deep suspicion. This is nothing new, but I'm desperate. The seats are filling, my homework page isn't. "Can you give me a sentence for 'shrew'?"

Before she can answer, Junior plows into the room with one finger jammed knuckle-deep up one side of his nose, announcing himself with a belch. He's a tall, skinny, shaggy-headed bulldozer. And, yeah, at times he's not wrapped too tight, but he's still a decent kid. He just loves the attention that comes from grossing people out. At least lately.

"Samuel Charles Hector Junior," Mr. McNab states without raising his voice. He sounds bored. Jacks swears that McDrab has been teaching since the Stone Age. "Chuck. You're late again," the man adds in his usual monotone from behind his desk, wearing the same sagging gray pants and brown corduroy jacket that he always wears. He peers at Junior over the top of thick, dark-rimmed glasses. No wonder Cheets nicknamed him "McDrab." "Mr. Hector, kindly remove your finger from your nasal cavity and find your seat before I am forced to give you a detention."

Junior growls something under his breath. He knocks a chair out of his way and then lumbers down the aisle at my left, shoving desks. For him, seventh grade has been about challenging and collecting detentions. He gets out of most of them, though. Teachers cut him breaks. They know that he didn't used to be obnoxious. Like the rest of us, they suspect that his life at home isn't great.

As he gets close to me, Gina opens her book and practically sticks her head inside it. Good-bye, vocabulary sentence. Maybe I can catch Katz before language arts. He always does his homework and is always generous about giving up a few sentences.

Junior stops at my desk and crosses his arms over the faded and cracked print on the concert T-shirt that he's been wearing almost every day of the school year. I wrinkle my nose, but don't ask him if he forgot how to use soap. "Morning, Junior." I tip my head.

Calling him Junior instead of Chuck should get me punched in the head. Especially since I encourage Jacks, Cheets, and Katz to call him that, too. But since he's a sort-of member of our posse, I get away with this. He used to be on the hockey team, but at the end of last season he got booted for too many major penalties. He got banned from the All-Stars Rink for too much challenging and too much butt-ending and jabbing other players with his stick.

Junior and I go back to fifth grade. He'd just moved into town when I caught him about to shoot a bottle rocket at the Buckner house. The old silver Cadillac that belonged to Mr. and Mrs. Buckner wasn't in the driveway, which meant that M. K. had to be home alone. Everyone knows he never leaves the house during the day. *Hey, what are you doing?* I asked Junior. *Don't be a jerk. Leave that Buckner guy alone.* At that exact moment, a low chuckle slipped out of a Buckner window on the second floor. The way Junior's spine went straight and his eyes bugged out told me that he'd heard it, too. We bolted. A block later we dropped onto Schmidt's lawn. We laughed so hard that we nearly peed in our pants.

"I blew away a doe yesterday," he tells me in his dry and raspy voice. A smirk pinches his face. His nut-brown eyes twinkle under tangled strands of straw-colored bangs.

I pull back from his dirty breath, hating how much he enjoys killing. Picturing a sweet-faced doe laid out lifeless turns me clammy. "You're only allowed to hunt antlered deer now."

Junior snickers. "Is that right?"

I hold myself back from flying out of my seat to shove him away from me. I don't need a one-way ticket to Principal Stack's office for roughhousing. The Stack Attack wouldn't care that Junior had murdered.

He pokes his nose-picking finger into my shoulder. "My first day out hunting and I blow away a doe." He grins big, puffs up as big as a skinny kid can. "Impressive, huh? I know what you're gonna say. It's good to be me, man."

"Yeah, those were my exact words," I mutter with plenty of sarcasm. No point in reminding him that hunting on Sundays is illegal in our part of Pennsylvania. He knows.

"My old man said he's never seen a hunter blow away an animal as easily as I did. I put a bullet right through the girl's chest. You should have seen the blood splatter."

I squirm. Any minute, my half-digested pizza breakfast will splatter.

Junior lifts his chin, jabs his thumb into his chest. "I'm a natural hunter, like my dad."

I nod, but the part of me that's Junior's friend wants to beg him not to be like his father.

Still, Junior's words burn. Because I'm not like my dad.

I couldn't pull the trigger of Granddad's gun when I had the chance to shoot a buck. I didn't impress Dad the way Junior had impressed his father.

"I gut the doe right there in the woods. I take my old man's eight-inch knife." Junior lifts an imaginary blade. "And slice through the belly." As if he's dissecting the poor animal all over again, he pulls the invisible knife down the deer's center. "I yank out the steaming intestines with my hands." His mouth makes a squishing noise. He sprays spit. "Steaming blood and guts are everywhere, man."

Two nearby girls glare at Junior, muttering something that includes "gross" and "pig."

"Shot a doe illegally. Good for you, Junior," I say in my most sarcastic tone.

He stiffens. "My old man told me that you and your old man went hunting, too. What'd you shoot, Tags? An itty-bitty mousie?" He asks this last question in baby talk.

My attention goes to my paper.

"Or didn't you shoot anything? Maybe you got buck fever." He throws his head back and laughs too loud, begging for a beating.

The slow shuffle of McDrab's sensible shoes keeps me from stuffing my notebook down Junior's throat. "Mr. Hector," McDrab says, sounding worn out. He waits, his droopy eyes peering over the top of his thick glasses. Again.

Junior grunts as he moves to the desk behind me. It

doesn't matter that he's bony, he still lands on the seat with the dull thud of a wet sack of sand.

By some miracle, he keeps his mouth shut during the rest of the class. We don't get in trouble for a change. But as soon as McDrab gives us five minutes to read some passage, Junior's chair creaks. He leans forward. "My old man says he's never been as proud as when I put a bullet through that doe." His words are hot claws against my bad ear.

"I'm sure," I tell him to keep from bruising his overripe ego again. But I turn down the volume on my hearing aid. I focus on McDrab as he scratches page numbers onto the board. Even from across the classroom he smells of his mentholated cough drops. "For homework, read these pages and answer questions—"

The bell rings. Books slap closed and chair feet scrape. I'm out of my seat. No page numbers. I'll get them from someone later. Now all I want to do is ditch Junior's hunting talk.

The hall outside the classroom fills. I almost run smack into Carrie Douglas. "Hey, Carrie." I flash my most charming grin. "Can I get the homework assignment from you?"

"Sure, Joey," she says in her sweet voice. She gives me a smile. Score.

We're not even three steps down the hall when a big hand comes down onto my right shoulder. "You want to hear how I skinned that doe, Tags?"

Carrie's top lip curls up. "Got to go, Joey. See ya." She is gone before I can get McDrab's assignment.

I know how she feels. "What died in your mouth, Junior?" I wave away his putrid breath.

"'What died in your mouth, Junior?'" he mimics in a too-high girl voice, as if that's how I sound. "Bite me. Now tell me what you shot on Saturday. My old man said your old man spent Friday night bragging about what a good hunter you'd be."

I spin around to face him. "What?"

"Yeah. At the Hunter's Inn."

People whip past us, calling my name, trying to joke. I don't move. I can't. "My dad was bragging about me?"

"You know how it goes. The old hunters hanging out before the season starts, swapping stories, talking big, getting psyched about opening day of buck season."

I nod, drag myself down the hall. Pictures of Dad perched on a stool in the murk and darkness of that bar flash in my head, in between images of his Saturday disappointment.

"Your old man is sure that you'll shoot a buck," Junior says as he tails me. "He bet my old man that you'd take one down before me." Junior laughs in snorts.

I stop again, stagger as I turn to face him one more time. I'd put him in a headlock if I wasn't caught off balance. "What? He made a bet?"

"He thinks you can shoot Old Buck." Now Junior tosses

his head back and guffaws as if he's never heard anything funnier. "He said you could track a deer better than a hunting dog." Junior bends over, holding his scrawny middle and snort-laughing even louder. Jerk.

"He bet on me?"

Junior shrugs. "Yeah. But don't sweat it. I don't think your family's life savings is riding on you shooting a deer, Tags."

But betting on me is too much. What will Dad say to his friends now? *I was wrong about my son. He didn't pull a trigger when he had a buck in his sights. He's a huge disappointment.* I can almost hear his buddies laughing. This is not what Dad needs. This is not what he goes to the Hunter's Inn for.

"My dad doesn't bet" is all I can get out of my mouth.

Junior shrugs right before the you'd-better-be-in-class bell clangs.

"Great. I'm late again." I take off. "Catch you later, Junior." I'm almost running down the hall now, hoping the Stack Attack doesn't ambush me. Still, I can't outrun the echo of what Junior had said. I can't escape the image of Dad, a guy who doesn't bet, bragging about me, thinking that he could rely on me.

I have to make him proud of me. I have to win this bet for him. And there is one way to do this right, to rock his world. My hand goes to the pocket at the front of my jeans, to the key that should be in the garage. Finding the right deer won't be the problem. I've tracked him a million times.

Tracking him to draw him has always been easy. But tracking Old Buck to shoot him will be the hardest thing that I have ever done.

By sixth-period study hall, a pasty dread has coated my insides.

"This game coming up is big," Cheets is saying as I slide into the chair at the desk in front of him. As laid-back as he is off the ice, he's a super-competitive goalie. In front of the net, he taunts opponents, calls them butt heads and goobers. He doesn't care that he's short. He's stocky and strong. He's told teammates to cram their hockey sticks when there's been lip about guarding the goal.

Cheets closes his round eyes, shakes his head in slow motion. He pushes one hand through his coal-colored, ruler-straight hair. "Dudes, that Jersey team has a killer forward line."

"Typical goalie," I say. "Always worrying about the attack."

"No worries. We've got Tags." Jacks tips his head at me. "The best center in the league."

"Keep it down," Katz snaps from a desk across the aisle from Cheets. Katz's gangly body is slumped over his math book. "We're not supposed to be yakking."

Jacks glances at me, his expression asking, *Do you believe this guy?* He jerks his thumb at Katz. "Mr. Follow the Rules is getting all worked up again."

"Careful, Jacks, you might get a detention for talking to me," I mock in a girl voice.

He cracks up.

Katz stops gnawing on his latest pencil. "Shut up."

We snicker. He stews. Even Cheets laughs.

"Speaking of the Jersey game." I get serious. "I got to miss practice today."

Jacks loses his smirk. Cheets goes pale. Katz bites through his pencil. All three stare at me, waiting for a punch line.

I shrug. "Duty calls. I got to do something for my dad."

"Oh, yeah, act like blood is more important than hockey," Jacks says. Mr. Sarcasm. A real stand-up comedian. He leans toward me. "Not kidding now, Tags. We got to get serious about this game with Jersey. We've only got a few weeks. We need you at practice."

"Sorry. I hate missing it." This should be obvious. These guys understand better than anyone that hockey is my life. I love the sound of skate blades cutting ice. I live to chase a puck, smack it past a goalie. I crave the feel of Flyer in my gloves. On the ice, my hearing aid doesn't matter. I make up for not being tall or broad by being fast and agile. These guys know that I dream of going pro and ending up in the Hockey Hall of Fame. I grab a pencil and open my notebook to avoid the disappointment coming my way. I start drawing Cheets as a maniac goalie.

"Tags, man, you miss three practices within a month

before a big game and Coach won't let you play." Katz drops the pencil pieces and pushes one hand over his short brown hair, which is always sticking up. "That's the rule."

Of course I know this, but what am I supposed to do? I've only got this afternoon and four more days to make things right. "I got to do something for my dad," I repeat.

"Katz has a point, dude," Cheets tells me. "We can't lose you."

"Yeah, I got that," I snap.

Jacks watches my face. He reads me. I let him. Best friends do this.

"I'll give Coach a good excuse," he finally says.

I nod my thanks.

"But I owe you a beating for this," he adds.

That's when I know we're good. I grin, grateful that these guys are cool enough not to ask about what I have to do.

CHAPTER 7

MONDAY AFTERNOON

Hunting vest on? Check. Dad's jacket on? Check. Four pairs of socks layered under Dad's laced-up boots? Check. Hunting knife in its sheath and on my belt? Check. Ammunition in the jacket pocket? Check. Beef jerky in the same pocket? Check. Hat and gloves in the opposite pocket? Check. I have everything I need. Except—

I boot-clomp back to my bedroom and over to my dresser. My fingers go to Mrs. D's digital camera, brush the sketch-book that it's sitting on. These pages are almost filled with my pencil and charcoal animal drawings based on photos that I've taken. Even though today has to be about hunting only, it's tempting to take the camera. Too tempting. I shove it into the jacket pocket. Note to self: Return the camera to Mrs. D the next time I see her.

Back in the hunting room, I grab Granddad's gun. Once upon a time, just thinking about going against Dad's rules would get me grounded without television privileges. But rules won't matter once I lug home the carcass of Old Buck. Dad's face will go bright the second he sees my kill. I picture him too thrilled about winning the bet to care about anything else.

Check.

The bang of the kitchen door swinging open, hitting the wall, and then slamming shut shoves me back into reality. "Little Brother?"

Philly! Crap! My life is over if she catches me dressed and primed to hunt.

"Joey?"

There is zero time to shed my jacket, vest, boots, gun, and knife. And the hunting room door is wide open, giving Eagle-eye Phil a clear view of me.

"No empty bags of Joey's junk food lying around. Maybe he didn't come home. Wait. There's Flyer." Phil growls. "There is no way that my worm brother went to hockey practice without Flyer."

Phil's sneakers pad across the kitchen tiles, moving toward the hunting room. "I owe you a burger and fries for the ride over here."

Heavier, shuffling feet follow her steps. Keys jingle. "Make it a Big Mac, large fries, and a shake, and I'll drive you to Hawaii and back," says a laid-back and mellow guy's voice. Jeebs.

Every instinct in my body screams, *Hide!* But where? I

grab Granddad's gun and move as fast as I can in Dad's boots to the closet with the sliding doors.

Philly sighs with loud frustration. "All day I've had these itchy suspicions that my weasel brother is going to hunt on his own this afternoon."

As her steps move closer, I cram myself to the darkest side of the closet, where the door is shut. I mash my spine against the back wall.

"How could your brother go hunting? Don't you have the key to your dad's gun closet?"

"Joey could find a way to get his hands on a rifle. The kid is sneaky. And, he's been working a serious rebel attitude." Her sneaker bottoms squeak against the wood floor of the hunting room. She gasps. "The door of the gun closet is open!" Phil growls low.

"Whoa," Jeebs mutters.

"My dad never leaves a door or drawer gaping, especially not one to a compartment of weapons," Phil says. "Joey, the slob, however, never closes doors. And my granddad's gun is missing. My brother is dead."

I hold my breath.

"What I don't get," Phil goes on in her thinking-out-loud tone, "is how the dork got into the locked closet when I've still got the key."

I picture her hand going to the slit pocket at the hip of her sweatpants, her fingers searching for the hard outline of that key.

Phil's sneakers scuff closer to me. With only a sliding door between us, I freeze. But sweat prickles at the back of my neck. The door farthest away from me pulls back, slow. Phil's hand pokes into the closet. My legs itch to jump up and bolt for my life. But in Dad's boots? Outrunning a cheetah would be easier. The end result would be the same—a bloody shredding.

Her fingers push the plastic hanger that held the jacket that I am wearing. The hanger swings, hits the back wall of the closet. "The coat Joey wore last Saturday is also missing." Phil's tone is low and dripping venom. "The boots are gone, too."

"The little dude really is out hunting on his own. That's brutal."

Little dude? Is Jeebs kidding?

The closet door smashes closed but bounces back open. "Come on," Phil snarls at Jeebs.

Sneakers stomp back into the kitchen. The shuffle follows. But all four feet stop when the telephone rings, loud and demanding. Three rings before the answering machine picks up.

"Hi! It's Mom," she announces in a revved-up and high-pitched voice after Philly's recorded *The MacTagerts aren't home, but leave a message and we'll get back to you.* "I didn't think anyone would be home, but when I called yesterday, I didn't get a chance to ask about how Joey's first day of hunting went. I didn't want you-all to think that I'd forgotten about it and—"

"Mom?" Phil's must-find-and-kill-*Joey* tone transforms into syrup. "Hi! Listen, I don't know how Joey's first day of hunting went," she stammers. Yeah, she is pretty much the worst liar ever. "But I'm sure Joey doesn't mind that you didn't ask him about it as long as you asked about hockey." Philly forces out a nervous snicker that makes her sound like a spastic mouse.

Jeebs starts humming "Love the One You're With."

"Sure, I'll tell him that you called back to ask about his big day."

Great. How am I supposed to tell Mom about Saturday without making Dad out to be a total jerk? If I tell her that I didn't shoot a buck, she'll ask about his reaction. If I say that I shot a deer, this will get back to Dad. And he's not a big fan of butchering the truth.

"Sure, Mom. No, it's okay. I've got to go, too," Philly says. "Love you." The phone clatters hard as she stuffs it back onto its base.

"You can't believe how rushed and preoccupied she is," my sister tells Jeebs. "But happy." She sighs. "This is awful, but I hate her being that happy. The second those Zuckermans called for her, she couldn't wait to get off the phone."

"They need her." I picture the purple knit hat on Jeebs's head bobbing.

"True," Philly says. "But maybe we need her more. It's cool that she's got this job where she's important and traveling and all that, but this family is not handling her being gone the way Dad said we would. He is lonely and depressed, Joey is out trying to be something he's not, and this house is ready to be condemned by the board of health."

"Intense," Jeebs says, his voice hushed. "Does your mom know about all this?"

"No. Believe me, I'd love to tell her not to picture life around here bouncing merrily along, but my dad doesn't want us to pressure her. He wants her to be here from wanting to be home, not having to be home."

"Wow. That's either amazingly selfless or incredibly stupid," Jeebs says as they cross the kitchen.

"Let's get out of here," Phil snaps. "But I'm going to kick my brother's rump from here to Taiwan when I catch him hunting." The back door opens and then slams shut.

Slow and steady, I slide open the door on my side of the closet. Inch by inch I remove myself with Granddad's rifle from my hiding spot. Instinct tells me to go for the front door, sneak out, and cut through fields and yards to get to Dewey's woods. But what if Phil heads for these woods, too?

I move into the kitchen, lean the rifle against the counter. Claude, doing his best impression of a fur doughnut beside the coffeemaker, where Mom doesn't allow him to be, yawns at me. He starts licking his butt.

I keep to the side of the window in the back door, behind

the curtain, watching my sister and Jeebs through the glass. My fingers go to the doorknob, turn it the tiniest bit, and pull. The door cracks open. Cold hits my face.

"If Joey went into the woods again with a gun, he's going to be sorry." Phil kicks at the driveway. Jeebs leans against the minivan, stroking its hood as if he's petting a kitten.

"Philly!" Mrs. Davies drops a bag of birdseed near the front of her house and then waves her arms windshield-wiper style. This works since her smile is as wide as a windshield. Philly flips a hand in a quick hi. It comes with a forced grin. Body language for *Hello but leave me alone. I need a distraction the way I need a broken ankle.*

"Honey, wait a sec!" Mrs. D rushes across her leafless lawn at Phil and Jeebs. With her elbows sticking out, the woman looks like a chicken trying to take flight. I almost bust out laughing. As she gets to her blacktop driveway, she slows and reknots her hair. "I need to talk to you about Joey."

My eyes zero in on Phil, sending her don't-tell-Mrs.-D-that-I'm-hunting telepathic messages. Just the thought of my sister blabbing makes me sweat marbles.

"Joey?" Philly's spine goes as straight as one of my pencils. "Did you see him this afternoon, Mrs. Davies?"

My insides do a roller-coaster drop to my toes.

"No, but—" Mrs. D steps closer to the van, her fingers fussing with the countless strands of black and turquoise beads hanging over her baggy brown sweater. "Philly, you've seen his animal drawings, right?"

Jeebs cuts off his humming. "Animal drawings?"

"Philly, your brother has a gift."

"He's got a gift, all right," she snarls.

Mrs. D presses her palms together prayer fashion in front of her chest. "But, he isn't enthused about that art show in Philadelphia. I don't think he understands what a great opportunity it could be for him." Mrs. D stops fussing with her necklace. "Maybe you could talk to him, encourage him. He listens to you."

Uh, no, I don't. I'd take advice from old Winston before I'd listen to my sister.

"Mrs. Davies, I'd love to see Joey concentrate on an art show, but I'm not sure how well focusing on drawing would go over with my dad. Joey can't even get his homework done." Phil starts for the passenger side of the van. "Now I've got to get back to cross-country practice."

"Yes," I whisper. "Go to practice! Go!"

Claude lifts his face, looks at me as if I'm something he's left behind in his litter box. "I don't need her tailing me," I tell him. As if I need to explain myself to an animal that licks his own butt.

"Believe me, Mrs. Davies, I'll be talking to Joey about his priorities. I can promise you that," Phil adds. "If I think of a way to get him interested in that art show, I'll let you know."

At least Phil doesn't spill that I'm all about becoming a

hunter right now. Giving her points for this, I turn, grab Granddad's gun, and go for the front door.

The knee-high yellow grasses of Dewey's meadow make shushing whispers as a breeze blows through them. Even though Dad drives here, the walk was calming and exactly what I needed. I suck in a lung full of cold air that carries the hint of smoke from a distant wood-burning stove. For a runaway second my mind forgets what I'm here to do. My whole being craves a pad and some pencils. But Granddad's gun, heavy in my hands, reminds me to forget about Mrs. D's art show talk. *You have to be a hunter,* I tell myself.

I pause to find the sun, check my bearings. The minute Philly and I were able to understand the difference between north, south, east, and west, Dad trained us to pinpoint the position of the sun in the sky to keep from getting lost and to gauge the time of day. Already the sun is sinking in the west. Some hunters might push their luck, stay in the woods until after dusk. Not this kid. Too many rumors of a prowling M. K. Buckner have me too freaked.

Short on time, I jog over frozen mud ruts left by truck tires. I'm zeroed in on the thin path that Dad and I followed this past Saturday. The air turns colder as I step into the shade of the scruffy evergreens and skyscraping eastern hemlock, birch, sycamore, and oak trees.

As I make my way to the blind, my mind rewinds to a

Sunday afternoon this past summer when Dad took Philly and me out here. A trip meant more for my sister than for me. Everyone always assumed that I would hunt. MacTagert fathers and sons probably went after mammoths with stones. But Dad would have loved to have Philly get into hunting, too, so that they could share time outdoors, in the woods. His favorite place in the world. He wanted to teach her all he knows about nature and the precision of tracking and shooting. Never mind that she marches around the house chanting, *Hunting is cruel and unfair to animals,* Dad had to show her the new blind. When she didn't get gooey over it, he finally gave up hoping. *At least,* he said, *we still have our mutual love of running and track.*

A twig cracks in the distance. Far-off vines and bramble rustle and crunch. A rabbit darts across the trail behind me. Yeah, one or more people are plowing through underbrush. But who? Only Dad and a couple other hunters have permission to hunt on the Dewey's property. Would Phil be stupid enough to come looking for me in these woods during hunting season?

The bang of a gun shatters the air. A pheasant catapults into the open from her hiding place under a bush.

"Hey! I'm a fifteen-year-old sophomore over here, not a deer," Philly shrieks, following Dad's instructions to call out if caught in the woods with a hunter firing off shots.

My heart starts thudding, pounding in my ears. Should I call out to her?

More branches, leaves, and underbrush snap, crush, and rustle. Sloppy cursing in a deep and snarling man-voice follows. I think I might recognize that voice. I hope not.

"I heard something up ahead," a younger, raspy-voiced boy calls out. Junior. Which means the snarly voice has to belong to Sam Hector.

Are they out here to win the bet? Did one of them shoot at Philly? But the Hectors don't have permission to hunt in these woods. Word is Mr. Dewey doesn't like or trust Sam.

"If it breathes, put a bullet into it. Deer, rabbit, squirrel. I don't give a crap," Sam says. "Practice makes perfect." He spits full force.

There's no way I am hanging back while my sister gets shot at. Going from tree to tree, I make my way toward the voices until I get close enough to see Sam bust into a small clearing that Philly is in. Even though he's not wearing any of the fluorescent-orange hunting gear required by the Pennsylvania Game Commission, one of his hands is wrapped tight around the barrel of a shotgun that I'm guessing is still warm from the recent shot. He's probably reloaded, too. Sam's other hand strangles a beer can. Dad would blow a fuse.

I am about to go to Philly when I look closer, see that Sam is shoulder slumped, pale, and winded. He looks like a bag of potatoes with legs, not as threatening as I first thought. My sister stands across from him, her hands on her hips, staring him down.

"Do I know you?" He squints at her. A loud and wet

belch erupts from him. It practically shakes the trees. "What do you want, missy?" He steps toward her, swaying.

A Canada goose and its mate, flying overhead, start honking. Phil almost leaps out of her sweats. She eyes Sam's gun. She shifts and steps in place like a little kid who needs to find a bathroom. The nervous energy coming off of her is enough to put a man on the moon.

I should go to her.

"I was letting you know that I'm not an animal that you can shoot at, sir," my sister says, lifting her pointy chin at Sam.

My heart rate triples, like I'm in sudden death overtime and I've got the puck. But instead of going for the shot, I freeze. Why did Phil have to come out here and then use a sassy tone with Sam? It's pretty common knowledge that he doesn't have a lot of patience these days.

He stares at her with a confused, twisted expression that seems to wonder if she's from another planet, which she kind of is, but that's another issue.

"Dad?" Junior's voice bounces off of the trees. "Where'd you go?"

Sam's body wavers. He turns his back to my sister and staggers off toward Junior's questions, mumbling something about how Philly can go to hell.

She takes off in the opposite direction. I deflate, breathe relief, certain that now she'll get her twiggy self back to the high school and cross-country practice. Finally. There's no way she's dumb enough to stay out here after running into Sam.

I take another route to avoid the Junior and Sam traveling show, trying not to crunch or shuffle the carpet of bronze-colored leaves while moving toward Dad's blind. But with each boot step, one question keeps repeating inside my brain: What would Dad have done if he'd seen Sam confronting Philly? The answer stings. He wouldn't have stayed still.

I am not inside the blind for more than a minute when leaves crunch louder than cornflakes. "Little Brother?" Velcro tears. Phil pulls the flap door back until I am staring at her shrunken, angry eyes. The rest of her expression says she's imagining how to maim me.

"Get lost," I tell her.

She yanks her cell phone from the side pocket of her sweatpants, flips it open, and presses it to the side of her head. "Hello, Dad? Joey is in Dewey's woods, hunting by himself."

"You're a jerk," I whisper even though I know that she didn't push Dad's speed dial number.

Her eyebrows arch at Granddad's gun. "Didn't I tell you not to hunt?" She plants her hands on her hips.

"Didn't I tell you to keep your nose out of my business?"

"I don't have your nonsense built into my schedule, Joey. I've already missed most of today's practice, thanks to you." She levels one finger, points it to the space between my eyes. "The next time you try and hunt on your own, I'll make sure Mom and Dad find out about it. You'll be grounded for so long that you'll forget how to lace up your hockey skates. You'll miss that Jersey game that you and your pals can't stop talking about."

The knuckles of my right hand turn white on the gun barrel. "Back off, Phil. You don't have a clue how it feels to disappoint him. You with all your ribbons and trophies." Without giving her a chance to respond, I push out of the blind and take off down the path.

Of course she comes after me. "Okay, it's true. Dad is most comfortable with what he knows. And that's track. My wins remind him of his days as a track star."

I don't glance back at her. My pace kicks up a notch.

"Hockey season conflicts with hunting season and the holiday catering rush at the hotel," she adds, repeating Mom's explanation. "He has more time in the spring to go to the track."

"He makes time for what he likes best," I mumble.

"Come on, Joey." She picks up her pace to keep up with me. "Let's get out of here."

Get out of here? I slow down, let her stride ahead of me. No. I can't leave. I haven't even aimed at one deer. "I'll catch up."

She jerks in a sudden stop, whips back around. "Did

you not hear the gunshot a few minutes ago? You have no idea how dangerous it is to be out here right now."

Uh, yeah, I do. "Gunshots are part of hunting season," I tell her in my best casual. I shake my head, acting as if I am amazed by her stupidity.

"Really, Joey? And did you know that a drunk and stupid Sam Hector happens to be the clown who shot off that gun? Believe me, in his condition, he couldn't tell the difference between you and a deer if his life depended on it."

When I don't answer, her hands go to her hips. "If you don't care about Sam Hector, then at least get your tail in gear to avoid that Buckner guy."

Okay, this gets my attention.

"The sun is going down." She glances up at the sky, then back at me. "You know what people say," she continues, taunting. "M. K. Buckner comes out here at night."

Her tone is fake spooked, but it still sends fear rippling up my spine. A feeling that doesn't blend with the disappointment swelling under my rib cage. Disappointment labeled "Joey's second trip into the woods without an antlered buck to show for it." And "Joey the wimp who didn't stick up for his sister." The fear makes my feet hot to move in double time toward home, but the disappointment is bigger. I'm not leaving yet.

But then a gunshot splits the air. Someone yell-curses in the distance. Sam.

"Come on, Joey." The taunt is gone from my sister's voice.

But I'm already stomping past her, still tingling with M. K. Buckner fear but more freaked now by the huge threat of a mean drunk.

And bloated with uselessness.

I need my pencils.

CHAPTER 8

TUESDAY, THE FOURTH DAY

My fingers rake a clean but crumpled T-shirt and flannel button-down out from under my bed. If Phil does laundry when Mom is gone, she dumps my clothes on my mattress. No folding. No putting anything away the way Mom does. Shirts, jeans, socks, and underwear fall on the floor and slide under my bed, mix with my stash of soda cans, bags of chips, and packages of beef jerky. Not that I care. Except that this reminds me that Mom isn't around, that she won't be entering my room, sighing and shaking her head at the mess. Reason number two hundred why I'm beginning to hate those Zuckermans.

The shirts drag over a bowl and a spoon that might be stuck to the rug. Cereal leftovers from two nights ago, which means that today is Tuesday. The fourth day of deer season. Only four afternoons left to bring home a buck.

But before I can deal with hunting, I've got to do the

homework that's due today. It would have been finished last night if I hadn't been drawing from the second I got home until about two a.m. Sketching Old Buck. Again. Drawing takes me to my comfort zone. All I have to think about are the images that flow from my head to my fingers. Instinct guides me. Last night, as the pencils sang, I settled and relaxed. Eventually I considered sleep. Not stepping up to help Philly in the woods and then blowing another opportunity to shoot a buck when I turned wimp stopped haunting me.

I step over dirty socks and wads of underwear. My sneaker crunches a bag of cheese puffs, but no social studies book. Where is it? As I stick my hearing aid into my left ear, about ready to give up on the idea of homework, my toe lifts a hockey shirt. Score! I grab the textbook and head for the kitchen. Twenty minutes to eat and do homework.

The second the bedroom door creaks open, I hear Dad's gravelly morning voice. Adjusting my hearing aid, I take slow steps through the living room, measuring his mood.

Dressed in his work clothes, a jacket and tie, he sits slumped over at the kitchen table with his broad back to me. One of his hands is at his side, one finger rubbing under Claude's chin as he purrs in a deep rumble.

My nose picks up the burn of toast, the brew of coffee, and the sour rot of ripe garbage. The burn means Philly, who is scooping dry grounds into the coffeemaker for a second pot, tried to cook breakfast. The stink reminds me that I forgot, again, to take the garbage out.

Dad's cologne, with a hint of Mom's clean linen perfume in it, greets me as I step into the kitchen. It's amazing that he isn't grumbling about the garbage odor. He's too busy squinting at creased pages and envelopes with windows for addresses. His forehead is wrinkled. Gray-blue shadows hang under his eyes. His World's Best Dad mug, half-filled with steaming black, is within his reach. The topless aspirin bottle sits beside the morning newspaper, which is still in a clear plastic sleeve. Weird. Dad usually reads the paper before doing anything else.

His mouth doesn't smile or frown when he tips his pale face up to me. "Morning, son. How'd you sleep?"

Out of habit, I turn my body to keep him from seeing my hearing aid. "Good." This back-to-normal chat doesn't feel natural with me still stuck in Saturday. "What are you doing?"

Philly stops scooping coffee and glares at me.

"Paying bills." Dad drops his pencil and drags his palms over his face. "They're overdue." He kind of groans. "Your mom called yesterday and asked me to deal with them. Seems R. Z. and Zinnia are talking about extending their damn trip."

Philly and I exchange quick, tense glances. Dad never used to curse. Not even "damn."

He reaches for the aspirin bottle. It rattles as he tips it to his palm, throws a few tablets into his mouth, and chases them with coffee. "I don't have time to deal with bills, but the phone, electric, gas, and satellite dish companies don't care." His mug comes down hard on the table. Claude bolts. Even Dad jumps a little, as if he startled himself. "The people at the bank don't care if there's enough hours in a day to do all there is to do around here. They want the mortgage payment on time." He rubs at his swollen eyes. "We had a routine, a rhythm around here," he adds, more to himself than to Philly and me. He glances at his watch and pushes back his chair. "I've got to get to the hotel. I booked a big conference and I've got a mountain of paperwork that has to get filled out this week. Otherwise, I'll be spending Saturday in the office. Hunting day. The one thing I look forward to lately."

Dad doesn't look at me as he says this. Ouch. If Phil opens her trap about me hunting on my own, she's dead.

"Come on, Joey," she growls instead, grabbing a nutrition bar, compliments of Mrs. D. "We have to get to school."

I don't argue that it's too early to leave and that I haven't had breakfast or touched any homework. I drag myself to the row of hooks beside the back door and drop my book. Do I grab my winter jacket, which doesn't fit me anymore? Or do I leave without it and hope Dad doesn't notice? But he's watching. I feel his attention. So I pull down the jacket, cram my right arm into a sleeve. It's a strangle fit. No surprise there. I barely got into the thing by the end of last winter. I push my left arm into the other sleeve. The material strains. My arms become unbendable.

"What's going on with that coat, Joey?" Dad's tension turns the air toxic.

The coffeemaker belches.

"Nothing." I reach toward the floor for the social studies book. *Rrrriiippp.*

I freeze. Dad's palms slam the tabletop, making the bills hop.

"I'm going to order Joey a new coat online," Phil says quick, turning to Dad.

He deflates, slumps in his seat. "Okay." He reaches for his back pocket and pulls out his wallet. His fingers flip it open, slide out a credit card. "Here." It lands with a small slap onto the table. "Your mother has a way of sniffing out bargains. Try to do the same, okay?"

Philly nods. I straighten. He stands, pulls on his wool coat. Phil and I step back as he heads for the door. "See you kids tonight," he mutters before stepping out into the cold.

Without letting the truck warm up for the usual five minutes, he throws it into reverse. The tires shoot gravel and leave rubber on Mercer Place.

"The bear is out of its cave again," Philly mutters.

No kidding. And it left before I got lunch money. Again. Lunches, like coats, sneakers, and bills, are not things that Dad is used to thinking about. "He'll be happier once he knows that we'll be hunting together on Saturday," I say while peeling myself out of the useless coat. I stuff my book into my backpack and leave, letting the door slam behind me.

"Happy morning, Joey!" Mrs. Davies calls and waves. By the time I get to her front door, she's pushing a foil-wrapped package at me. My nose recognizes fresh pastry. "Cinnamon raisin buns from Just Desserts," she announces.

It's hard not to drool. "Wow. Thanks, Mrs. D." I consider dropping to kiss her feet.

"You're more than welcome," she says. "I know you have to get to school, but stop by this afternoon." She pats my arm. "Bring what you've been working on."

My stomach sinks. I nod. How can I say no with bakery buns warm in my hands?

The second I am out of her sight, I rip back the foil and ram a bun into my mouth. Behind the cinnamon and butter, the pastry tastes of guilt. How many people can I disappoint? Dad. Philly. Mom. Mrs. D. I sigh as I reach the streetlight across from the Buckner house.

Of course the rest of the hockey posse hasn't arrived yet. Which means I get to stand here wondering if Man-Killer is sizing me up from a window. I lean one shoulder against the pole, going for casual. I whistle. As if being this close to M. K. Buckner doesn't scare the crap out of me. It should. Not even a year ago Cheets threw a rock at the house while Mrs. Buckner was out. Window glass shattered. I assumed that we'd knock on the door to apologize, but everyone ran. And Cheets doesn't run unless he's being threatened. With everyone gone, I lost my nerve. And probably got blamed by M. K. for the busted window.

I listen for the whine of door hinges, the creak of steps, and heavy breathing. I also tune in for the muffled classical music that sometimes drifts out slow and unexpected on the smoke that rises from the Buckner chimney.

My eyes catch a slight movement. A shade covering an upstairs window lifts. As I blink at it, it's yanked down quick. Was it lifted and then pulled back down by M. K. Buckner? Does he remember me from when Cheets broke that window? Or from when Katz threw the peanut M&M's at the house? Or does Man-Killer recall too many games of Ding-Dong Ditch when Jacks ran through the Buckner flower beds, a human Weedwacker.

"Hey, Tags!" Jacks, tossing his lucky puck between his hands, struts down the sidewalk.

Katz follows, his shoulders rounded and drooping. Part of a Pop-Tart crumbles in his grip. The stems of two bananas poke out of his jacket pocket. "What's up, Tags?"

Cheets cuts across the yard to the right of the Buckner place. He crosses 523, coming at us, a clod of dirt in his grip. "Anybody up for a Ding-Dong Ditch?" Grinning, he tips his head at the Buckner house.

These guys know that I've never been okay with pestering Buckner. I'm less okay with it since his mom died. Sure, I might have hollered, *Anybody home?* at the house a while back. Maybe twice. And, yeah, I've hurled a few candies at the place. But ringing the bell and running always felt wrong.

"A shade moved in a Buckner window. Not even two

minutes ago," I tell the posse, hoping this will scare them off the prank.

Jacks stops tossing his puck. Katz stops chewing. Six bugged-out eyes stare at me.

"Junior swears that he has new proof that the dude hunts for his food at night and eats it raw, right after the kill." Cheets nods to confirm this. "According to Junior, when Man-Killer goes out at night, he thinks he's in the jungles of Vietnam again, hunting the enemy."

These rumors never get stale.

Jacks rolls his eyes. "Where'd Boy Junior get that? The Science Fiction channel?"

"Here we go." Katz groans.

Jacks and Cheets are always battling over who has the latest Buckner scoop or story.

"Whatever," I say. "Man-Killer already blames me for that busted window. No more ringing his doorbell, throwing anything, or yelling at him. Get it?"

Katz shakes his head. "I never threw any rocks. Chocolate, yes. Rocks, no."

Jacks backs away from the Buckner house, trying to act like he's not freaked by it. "Why are you girls worried about him? As long as no one gets grabbed or buried under those porch steps—"

"Leave the guy alone," I tell them. I let a moment pass. "Keep bothering him and I'll make sure he gets pictures of you losers with your names and addresses written on the backs."

Jacks and Katz jump on me. We wrestle. I get Katz in a headlock. Jacks knuckle-rubs my skull. We're about to drop to the ground when Katz slips away from me.

"We're gonna be late," he announces, jumping up and glancing at the watch that his parents gave to him for his birthday. He's winded and his hair is sticking up more than usual.

"What about Junior?" Cheets scans the area, drops the dirt clod.

Jacks gets to his feet, hikes up his jeans, and then checks to be sure that he hasn't lost his lucky puck. "What's with him being late all the time this year?"

"His dad," Cheets tells us in a lowered voice. "Before Junior can leave for school, he has to make sure the dude is out of bed."

This quiets us. As we start for Jefferson Middle School, the image of Dad rolled in Mom's comforter, deep in a sleep coma, comes uninvited. If Mom keeps traveling all the time, am I going to have to deal with Dad the way Junior has to cope with his father?

I'm grateful when Jacks, Katz, and Cheets distract me by starting up about M. K. Buckner again. It's the usual: Does the guy only come out at night? Is he a man killer? Did he murder his mother? Did he bury her under the porch steps? I'd rather talk about hockey, but at least their jabber takes my mind off the possibility of my life turning into Junior's world.

Inside Jefferson, we separate into our classes. My day starts off with McDrab giving a pop quiz on the social studies homework that I never did. My head tells me that I should care. I've definitely failed this quiz. But my heart knows that I wouldn't have, couldn't have, given up thirty seconds of drawing Old Buck last night.

Once this season of antlered buck distractions is over, I'll concentrate more on school and homework. Really.

In my next class, Señora Zilton, "Zippy Zilton" to those of us who catch her napping during the videos on Latin America, gives me until the end of the day to *find* my Spanish assignment. If I don't, I'll earn a big, fat zero. Señora Zippy es un freako.

Thanks to her, I get a lecture during English. Ms. Greason doesn't appreciate me doing Spanish homework while she's discussing biographies. She wraps up her rant by asking me what I'm reading for the book report that's due next week. Good question.

By the time the bell rings, I'm out of my chair. Freedom or bust. Lunch is next. No pop quizzes. No missing homework. No reminders of stupid book reports. But as I'm heading for the door, Greason points at the questions she's written on the board. Questions to be answered in our book reports. Questions I didn't write down.

. . .

"Listen up." I saunter over to the hockey posse table in the back corner of the lunchroom. "Who's gonna give me the questions for Greason's book report?" I drop my soda can onto the table. A bag of cheese puffs and the mashed, foil-wrapped cinnamon buns follow.

Jacks checks out my meal. "The lunch of a champion."

Okay, sure, I'd rather have Mom's killer roast beef sandwiches and homemade slaw in front of me, but dreaming isn't going to make that happen.

Katz sniffs, turns away from the three bologna sandwiches piled in front of him. "What've you got there, Tags?"

"Check these out, boys." I peel back the foil, and the scent of cinnamon and sugar flavors the air. It doesn't matter that the buns are smashed. "One of these babies to the guy who gives me Greason's questions."

Cheets shrugs, forever laid-back when he's not in his goalie pads, ready to sacrifice his life to keep a puck out of the net. "I don't make deals with dudes who no-show hockey practices."

Jacks almost bites off his fingertips instead of his peanut-butter-and-grape-jelly sandwich. Katz almost blows milk out his nose. Classic.

Meanwhile, I'm sizing up the purple-and-blue bruise on Jacks's left cheekbone. How did I miss it this morning? Was I too distracted by M. K. Buckner? According to Katz, when the boys were getting in extra skate time after practice yesterday, Jacks hip-checked a high school defenseman. In return, Jacks caught a high-stick. I hate that I missed all that.

"Show up at hockey practice today, Tags," Jacks says after swallowing a huge PB&J bite. "And I'll consider giving you the book report questions." He grins, showing his braces, matted in peanut butter see-food. "I love a little blackmail with my lunch."

"You're disgusting." I laugh. "But whatever. I'll be at practice." And then I whip a cheese puff at his forehead. It nails him between the eyes.

The four of us fall over in hysterics and almost slide off our chairs. As Jacks wipes neon-orange powdered cheese off of his skull, Cheets glances back at the cafeteria double doors. "Dudes, whatever you do, don't say anything to Junior about him not showing up at the light this morning. His father made him go hunting last night until four a.m. He overslept and now he's got a detention for an unexcused absence from first period. His dad is going to go nuclear over that detention."

Is this what Junior and I have in common these days? Father and son hunting troubles and hassles in school? Nothing against Junior, but I am not liking the connection.

Katz hesitates before cramming a sandwich into his mouth. "Hunting at night is totally illegal." He'd know. His mom works in the offices of the Pennsylvania Game Commission.

"Hunting at night?" My shoulders hit the seat back. "They were spotlighting?" I don't want to picture them using flashlights to blind animals and then shoot them.

"That's beyond lame," Jacks puts in.

"It's unfair to the animals," I snap.

"Junior told me that his dad wanted to shoot a buck," Cheets says, lowering his voice and leaning toward the center of the table. "But even with the lights, he only shot a raccoon."

Katz sputter-laughs and spits bologna.

"No surprise," Jacks points out. "The guy can't see much out of one eye."

I shake my head the way Dad does when he talks about Sam's "unfortunate" accident.

"Junior's old man settling for a raccoon had nothing to do with bad vision." Cheets looks at each of us. "Junior said they ran out of Dewey's woods when M. K. Buckner showed up."

"Junior and his dad don't have permission to be in Dewey's woods," I say.

Katz rolls his eyes. "Tags, get with the program. My uncle Frank says Junior's dad brags nonstop about hunting in those woods."

Katz's uncle, who tends bar at the Hunter's Inn, also told him that Junior's dad has been practically living at the bar since he got laid off from his job, after his eye injury. Has Uncle Frank mentioned my dad being at the bar, too?

Katz swallows more sandwich. "Frank says a few beers

get Junior's dad jabbering about shooting the biggest deer in Bucks County. He doesn't care that he can't see well enough to shoot straight, he wants to prove that he's the best hunter around again."

Jacks lets go a snort. "Since when do the best hunters spotlight?"

"It rots that we can't prove that Junior's dad has been breaking laws," Katz says.

"We couldn't turn him in even with proof." Cheets shakes his head. "He's Junior's dad."

Before a debate gets going, Junior pushes through the cafeteria doors. They bang open. He storms toward our table, knocking into countless shoulders and chairs, getting multiple dirty looks in return. "Greetings, gentlemen." His skinny butt lands hard in his usual seat. He drops a plastic bag of cereal, his lunch, onto the table.

How far off am I from eating cereal from a bag?

"What'cha got there, Tags?" Junior's bloodshot eyes widen at the cinnamon buns.

Only a month ago he beat up a school vending machine for junk food. He almost got suspended. Yeah, it might seem like the kid has kitty litter for brains, but the truth is, he's angry. And scared. I get this.

"Nice," he says when I slide him my cheese puffs.

Cheets pushes what's left of his sloppy joe sandwich, today's hot lunch, over to Junior. The stuff has gone cold and reeks of dog food, but Junior doesn't care.

He starts cramming his mouth full of crumbling cheese puffs. "Did you guys hear how I blew away a doe this past Sunday?"

The scrape of my chair feet against the tiled floor screams that I'm in no mood for this hunting talk. "I'm out of here." I stand, glance at the wall clock. I grab my soda and Mrs. D's cinnamon buns. "Later, chumps."

Jacks and Junior give me dual thumbs-up. Cheets nods. Katz flips up a hand.

"By the light, after school," Jacks tells me.

As if I need to be reminded about where we meet before hockey.

"Last one there gets a beating."

"I'll be there." *Maybe.*

One period later, I'm in art class and in an excellent mood. There are zero criticisms in this room. No nagging, either. Mr. Leo, a guy who wears his graying hair in a short pony-tail, hangs out in museums, and paints portraits in his free time, practically slobbers on my work. Which means I score an easy A-plus in this class. This, of course, doesn't mean much to Mom and Dad. Mom would rather have As in math, English, or science. Whatever.

Carrie Douglas is in here, too. Another bonus. She sits only two seats away and when her gray-blue eyes check out what I work on, they grow wide. Sometimes she pushes her wavy brown hair behind her ears, to get a better look. Or, she asks me for help, which is almost as good as scoring points in overtime.

But science comes after art. And Junior comes with science.

I'm already in my seat when he plows into the room as his hand and armpit make loud gas noises. "Hey, MacTagert," he announces in his bullhorn voice as he approaches me, sliding his hand out from under his T-shirt. His grin is smug. "Did I tell you about my dad's plan to stun Old Buck so that I can blow him away?"

My lab partner, Jennifer Wilkenson, blinks her baby blues and scrunches her mouth into a pinched frown as she backs away from our table. This might have something to do with the way Prince Charming is wiping his wet nose on his forearm. Just for her.

"What's your dad going to do, blind Old Buck with bright lights?" My question snaps.

"Whoa!" Junior jerks and steps back from me. "No one said anything about spotlighting, Tags. Besides, only the big, bad M. K. Buckner goes into the woods at night. Right?" Junior throws his head back and cackles.

"Shut your trap, Junior." The words slide out cold.

"What's the matter, Tags? You afraid your old man's gonna lose that bet?"

I lean toward him, lower my voice. "Neither of you have permission to hunt in Dewey's woods. And my dad doesn't lose bets to cheaters."

Junior's expression loses all of its humor. Fear flickers in his eyes. "What are you getting all uptight about, Tags?" His tone drops, low enough for only me.

Ms. Peppers moves to the front of the room. As usual, her frown doesn't match her sunny dress, which reminds me of Mom's bright yellow, flowered laundry bag. "Mr. Hector." She plants her hands on her wide hips. "Will you be leaving class before it begins?"

"I'd rather not, ma'am," Junior answers in his most respectful tone.

Ms. Peppers, her hands still on her hips, turns to Jennifer. "Miss Wilkenson, find your proper place in the next ten seconds or you and Mr. Hector can visit Principal Stack together."

Just the possibility lands Jennifer on her chair seat in a heartbeat.

Junior's gaze lingers on me before he moves on. "Don't give yourself a wedgie over that stupid bet, Tags. Going after Old Buck isn't my idea. Sure, I'm into shooting, but I don't care what I nail. Deer, squirrel, or raccoon, they're all the same to me." His expression sags. "It's my old man who's worked up about Old Buck, especially now that there's a challenge. You know?"

He's gone before I say, *Yeah, Junior, I know.*

CHAPTER 9

FOUR AFTERNOONS LEFT

When I grab my latest sketch of Old Buck from the art room after school, to show Mrs. D, Mr. Leo starts yapping about how I *excel* in drawing real life, which apparently has him thinking about some student art exhibit at the town library. He wants me to display the drawing there. Yeah, like I need someone seeing it and telling Dad about it. In two minutes he'd tell Mom. They'd figure out that I put more time into art than into my other classes. Or into target shooting. Other hunters would want to know how I got close enough to Old Buck to draw him.

Even though I haven't stopped home to get my hockey stuff, I get to the streetlight at the usual time. My foot is kicking at its base when Jacks and Cheets round a corner, come toward me. Jacks is swinging his old hockey stick wide, as if he's about to ice a puck, shoot it the length of a rink. The stick is nicked and taped in about fifty places, but Jacks swears it brings him good luck. The same way he thinks the puck he carries brings him luck. My lips twitch, itching to ask how, with these double-duty charms, he ended up with a purple welt on his cheek.

As the guys get to me, Cheets digs a couple pennies out of his coat pocket. He squints, brings his arm back, aiming at the Buckner house.

"What are you doing?" I ask, even though I already know.

He freezes, shifts his eyes my way without moving any other muscle.

"Gonna break another window and then bolt? Gonna leave me by myself to apologize again?" I don't remind them that I never got past the Buckner gate with that apology. The scrape of what might have been an upstairs window opening paralyzed me. I hauled tail away from that house before M. K. could push the nose of a gun out of the window to aim at me.

Jacks pauses mid-swing. "What's the big deal if we throw a couple pennies at that house? Have you become Man-Killer Buckner's new pal or something?"

"Maybe his boyfriend." Cheets snickers. But at least Mr. Mature returns the pennies to his pocket.

"Or maybe I'm not in the mood to see the guy bothered." I glare at Cheets.

Jacks lets fly a slap shot, cutting the air with his stick. "Save the energy for the ice, boys," he says, quoting Coach.

"That reminds me." I hesitate. "I can't go to the rink right away this afternoon."

Cheets jerks his head right and then left, searching all around me. "Dude, where's your hockey stuff?"

Jacks's mouth flatlines. "Missing hockey again? No stinking way. What's up with you?"

The weight of having to miss another afternoon on skates gets heavier. What will Coach say about another no-show? Will he bench me for the Jersey game? My fingers pinch the edge of the large envelope that holds my sketch. Once I take down a buck, I can get back to the ice. I can start drawing again. "I got to do something for my dad."

Cheets studies the ground, shaking his head.

Jacks stares at me. "Is your dad making you study with tutors again?"

"No." Not like last spring when Mom and Dad sentenced me to hard labor with boring tutors. Something about getting me through sixth grade.

"Then come play hockey," Jacks says. "You live for it. Your dad knows that."

But he doesn't respect it, I don't say. I've never come right out and told these guys that my dad doesn't care much about hockey, doesn't find it as practical or as necessary as hunting. *A hockey stick won't put meat on the table,* he said at the beginning of the season this year, after I blew off target shooting to work on my slap shots. *Worry about playing hockey once you're in high school, when you can get a scholarship out of it.*

"Come on," Jacks prods. "Get your seat meat to practice this afternoon."

I shake my head. "I owe my dad." And there are only four afternoons left before Saturday.

"*Owe him?*" Jacks crinkles his forehead. "Owe him what?"

Being best friends doesn't mean that I have to explain how I'd disappointed Dad. But I should say something. "He wants me to be a hunter."

"Yeah. So?"

"So he made a bet with Sam Hector. I'm supposed to shoot a buck before Junior does."

"A competition." Jacks nods. This he understands.

"Intense," Cheets agrees. He gets the pressure of a competition. He also knows, from his dad, the value of venison in the freezer. But unlike my dad and Junior's father, Mr. Cheetavera doesn't care if Cheets hunts. He says that his son isn't ready to shoot deer. Not this year. The kid's aim is too unsteady and inconsistent. This is okay, though. Mr. Cheets doesn't see hunting as bonding time, the way Dad does. The Cheetaveras don't need the deer meat the way the Hectors do. Cheets's dad doesn't need his boy to help him track deer the way Sam needs Junior. Lucky for Cheets.

"Okay, fine, a competition," Jacks says, quick and dismissive. "Then go out with your dad on Saturday and shoot a deer."

Life would be good if the solution was this simple. Not even Cheets seems to catch on that if I don't prove that I'm a hunter before then, my dad won't ask me to join him on Saturday. "It's not that easy, Jacks." I can't admit to buck fever. Not even with these guys.

"Okay, Tags, your call. But you'd better show up at the rink when you're done. We'll be there late." Jacks punches my shoulder. This seals the deal.

"That works." Saying this out loud makes it so. And it has to be. I don't need Coach annoyed with me. He can't think that I'm not serious about the game.

Jacks lifts his stick again. "Okay. I'll give Coach an excuse about why you'll be late."

"Cool," I say.

"But I mean it, you'd better show up." He points his stick blade at my nose.

"Don't worry."

Jacks drops his stick. "Fine. I'll give you the book report questions then."

"Works for me," I agree, walking away. But this is a lie. Where am I going to find the time to get to the rink this afternoon?

With one last glance back at the Buckner place, I go straight to Mrs. D's house. To explain why I can't hang out with her, either.

"Winston adores you, Joey." Mrs. D is running her palm along the side of this old hound lying flat out and almost comatose in front of the fire crackling in the living room hearth.

"His snoring tells me that he's adoring that fire," I say, kind of snickering. That same fire is starting to make me sweat. If I don't peel off one or two sweatshirts, I might pass out. But I can't do any peeling since I can't stay here.

Mrs. D grabs the edge of the throw rug Old Winston is on and hauls it back from the hearth. Her bracelets jingle beside his ear, but the dog doesn't flinch. She pats the hip of the leg that's been cut off above the knee.

Your old man is sure you'll shoot a buck. He bet my old man that you'd take one down before me, Junior had said, snorting and laughing. Serious envy mixes with the dread that's pooling in my belly. Lucky Winston doesn't have to prove anything to anyone.

Mrs. D straightens and pads in her baggy socks over to the soft chair across from me. She brushes the wrinkles out of her wool skirt and Mr. D's button-down flannel shirt, which she's wearing as a jacket over her turtleneck. "Okay. Let's see what you've brought for me." She pulls small, oval reading glasses from Mr. D's shirt pocket, places them onto her nose, and then slides my drawing out from the envelope that I brought to her. Her humming mixes with the half-frozen rain that is beginning to tip-tap against the roof.

After a few minutes of staring at the Old Buck sketch,

Mrs. D puckers her lips as if ready to kiss the paper. "Joey, this is excellent."

"Thanks." I grab a cookie from the plate on the table in front of me. I bite, crunch, and sink deeper into the soft chair.

Until an engine belting out bursts of rumbling air and a movement on the other side of the picture window snag my attention. The Minivan of Death pulling away from my house. Sheriff Phil sits shotgun in the passenger's seat. And HA! Since I haven't been home yet, Granddad's gun is locked away. The hunting jacket and the boots are where they belong in the sliding door closet. Phil has to be going back to school convinced that I'm not hunting. Perfect.

"I have to go," I announce too loud as I hop to my feet.

"Yes, of course," Mrs. D says. "I'm sorry that you can't stay, but I understand. You're a busy guy." She gives me a wink, looks back at the Old Buck drawing. "It's amazing to me how you managed to catch the depth of expression in the deer's eyes."

"I drew that picture from a photo I took with your camera," I tell her.

She hums. "He must be used to you being near him. You've gained his trust."

I nod, wondering if he'd let me walk right up to him and aim a rifle at him.

"Imagine the work you might produce with more training, Joey. With art school."

My chest swells at the idea. An excitement ripples through my veins. This is the feeling I get when I'm about to slap a puck past a goalie. But I warn myself not to consider art school.

Mrs. D leans back, plucks the glasses off of her nose, and watches me. One of her fingers twirls the tangled strands of her necklace. Something in her eyes hints that she sees what I'm thinking. Her small, sympathetic smile tells me that everything will be okay.

I wish.

"Why don't we talk about your future as an artist at another time." As always, her tone holds no criticism, no judging. She leans forward and slides my drawing back into the envelope, making sure that it doesn't buckle and that the corners don't mash. Her smile stays soft as she rises from her chair with the envelope under her arm.

As I start for the door, she picks up a napkin and fills it with cookies. "How goes the hockey, Joey?"

What can I say? "We have a big game coming up," I offer.

She inflates. "How exciting. You'll have to tell me when and where. I'd love to go." At the door, she passes the envelope and the cookies to me and then pats my arm. "Come over anytime for an art lesson or a snack or to talk. Whatever you need."

The image of the second-floor art studio that she had built last summer fills my head. The sunshine that pours through huge windows and skylights keeps the place warm and bright. The scents of paints, pencils, pastels, inks, and paper perfume the air. A thick rug and lots of pillows make it even more comfortable. "Thanks, Mrs. D. I'll be back soon." I can hardly wait.

Within half an hour I'm decked out in hunting gear and stepping into Dewey's woods with Granddad's gun loaded and locked. My nose is dripping, but wiping at it makes the chapped skin underneath sizzle.

Everything is damp. Icy rain is falling in chunks and sliding off bonelike branches onto mats of decaying leaves. The smudged-gray sky is hanging low, tangling in the tops of the trees. The woods smell musty. The raw chill is penetrating and miserable.

But within three steps I pick up deer. Not a sighting, not a sound. Just a feeling. It pulls me northwest. "Don't get distracted," I whisper to myself. No thinking about M. K. Buckner or hockey. No fantasies about art school or picturing myself in Mrs. D's warm studio. This afternoon has to be about tracking and shooting.

At the edge of a soggy meadow, the compass needle inside me quivers. It points straight ahead. I slip behind a thick oak. Score! Four deer graze about fifty feet away. Three beautiful doe on spindle legs hanging out with a small, four-point buck.

My hand reaches for Mrs. D's camera, still in the pocket of the hunting jacket, but I stop myself. I drop to one knee instead. My thumb finds the hammer on Granddad's gun and brings it back slow. With the gun ready to fire, I push the butt of the rifle stock between my collarbone and armpit. My stomach double knots. Dad's voice fills my ears, guiding, instructing, insisting.

I shift left, maybe an inch, just enough to clear the oak. I set the gun sights on the heart of the buck. A clean shot. No problem. Except that my own heart has become a mass of fast thumping lead. My determination starts to melt, but I force my pointer finger around the trigger. *Picture that deer as a soup can, a stuffed horse, or one of Philly's dolls,* I tell myself.

A breeze whispers, *Shoot, shoooot.*

I hear Dad telling me to squeeze the trigger, but the gun barrel quivers. I shift, it knocks into the tree. The deer lift their heads. They stiffen, turn their faces to me. Four sets of huge eyes full of questions. Four tails that flick up to show the white undersides. Large, leaf-shaped ears move forward and back, unsure. Soup cans, stuffed animals, and dolls don't look afraid.

My throat tightens. I stop breathing. *Shooo—t,* the breeze urges the way Dad would. I gulp, line up the buck in the sights again. Granddad's gun weighs a ton now. My shaking finger is a boiled noodle on the trigger. Sweat pops out on the back of my neck and forehead.

In a blink, all the deer but one turn and leap into the tree shadows. The leftover doe stands frozen, too stunned to bolt, puffing out clouds of steam from her nostrils. "Get out of here!" My voice comes out without my permission. It cracks, wavers. "Run, you idiot!"

She jumps as if startled, finally gets a clue, and follows her friends. Chaotic twig snapping and brush plowing replace the silence.

The second that she disappears, warm relief spreads through me until Dad's voice rings in my ears, *Why didn't you shoot? What's wrong with you?* Junior's words follow, *My old man said he's never seen a hunter blow away an animal as easily as I did . . . I'm a natural hunter, like my dad.*

I turn away from the meadow, my feet jiggling in Dad's boots. I retreat into the shadows, wishing that they would swallow me. "Junior's a natural hunter, but I'm a natural wimp," I tell the trees. I almost wish Man-Killer Buckner would come along to put me out of my misery.

By the time I turn back to the clearing, my compass needle has settled, points at nothing. Charcoal-gray dusk is dropping over the trees, snuffing the murky daylight. Still, I find the path that the four deer followed. Maybe, just maybe I can get another chance at the small buck.

I'm not even halfway across the meadow when a buff-brown blur streaks across it about fifteen feet ahead of me. A rabbit that might as well have "Joey's last chance" written on it. In my head, Dad screams, *SHOOT IT!*

The rabbit pauses, as rabbits do. I lift my gun, chamber a round, and aim. *Don't think! Shoot!* Dad's voice booms in my ears. My finger squeezes the trigger.

The crack of the gun breaks apart the icy air. A piece of a second hangs. The rabbit drops. My jaw does, too. And my stomach. And my heart. The ripples of the explosion spread out in expanding rings through the sky and through my center the way water circles spread out from a dropped stone.

The barrel of Granddad's gun dips, points at the ground. My breath comes and goes in ragged scraps, but I force myself forward. The brown-and-tan rabbit with the white belly and ball tail lies flat out. It's large, handsome, must be a male. A buck. The wet red hole behind his front leg is from my gun.

I suck in a cold breath, desperate to take back what I've done. I drop to my knees, stroke the rabbit's face. It's warm, as if breath is still inside him. But his eyes are lifeless brown marbles with shock and fear frozen in their centers. The gnawing cold no longer matters. The darkness slithering in, surrounding us, no longer matters.

After I unload Granddad's gun, I force my fingers to the rabbit's back legs. I make my fingers grip them gently, as if the rabbit is sleeping and I don't want to wake him. The fur feels soft, almost feathery, over the bones. A thick sadness clots in my throat. What have I done?

I start home, the rabbit's body knocking against my right calf and knee. Each hit ripples up my thigh and rips through my center. My eyes fill and burn. But real hunters don't cry.

CHAPTER 10

TUESDAY EVENING

With each step closer to home, the rabbit bangs harder against my leg. Even though I'm counting the seconds until I can drop this carcass, I hesitate at the end of my driveway. Because watery yellow from the floodlight over the garage spills over the side of my house. And here comes my sister, down the concrete steps off of our kitchen, holding a large manila envelope.

I slide behind one of the two fat holly bushes at the end of our driveway, the shrub that is still mangled on one side from when Jeebs backed the van into it when he couldn't stop. As Phil moves toward Mrs. D's house, I adjust the volume on my hearing aid.

"Philly!" Mrs. D steps out of her garage and flings her arms wide. Bracelets jingle.

"Hi! I found something for you," I think I hear my sister say. She pushes the envelope at Mrs. D.

I'm pretty sure I can see Mrs. D's mouth drop open before a huge smile spreads across her face. "I knew you could talk him into it!" She claps twice.

Who is *him*? And what did Phil talk *him* into?

"Let's bring it inside," Mrs. D says.

Phil offers a painted-on clown grin, a sure sign that she's up to no good. Still, Mrs. D pats her back and herds her into the garage.

Just as I am about to bolt up the driveway, the garage door opens and closes. I drop down again. Philly jogs across our driveway, back to our house. The envelope has been replaced with a bunch of bananas, a bottle of that green slime juice, and a white bakery bag that is probably filled with carrot cake, my sister's favorite treat.

Once she disappears inside our house, I shoot one last glance at Mrs. D's garage. When I'm sure that she's not coming back outside, I make my move with the rabbit and the gun.

It's not easy, but once I get to the kitchen steps, I move almost without sound up to the back door. Peering through the window, I spot Claude on the counter doing his best impression of that Great Sphinx in Egypt. He's watching Philly with pure disapproval, but she doesn't seem to be doing anything suspicious.

"What he doesn't know won't hurt him," she says, as if answering the cat's criticism.

At least I think that's what she's said. Whatever. I hop

off the stoop and lay the rabbit gently down on the hard-packed dirt, in the pool of light from the bare bulb over the back door. I place Granddad's gun down behind me and kneel close to the long-eared body. As I slide the knife out of the sheath on my belt, my fingers and palms begin to crawl with an itching stickiness, as if the rabbit's fur is under my skin.

As I wipe my palms on Dad's hunting jacket, the back door flies open. In two steps, Phil is at the edge of the stoop, glaring down at me. "You weren't at hockey practice? You've been hunting again?"

No, this rabbit shot itself on our doorstep, I almost snap at her.

"I don't have time for this, Joey. It's already after five. I have to finish making dinner, I have a paper to write for English, a major quiz to study for, and my nails need polish ASAP."

For half a minute I don't look at her. But when I do, her anger dilutes. "Oh, Joey."

Her sympathy drills into my chest, brings on an intense ache. I stare at Dad's hunting jacket, wipe my hands against it, trying to keep the tears back. The canvas scratches.

"Joey." Phil heaves a mega-sigh. "What did you do?"

I force my attention back to the rabbit. "Don't bother reminding me that I'm not a hunter. I get it." My voice wavers. "I couldn't bring home a deer if it dropped dead on top of me."

When she doesn't whip a sharp reply back at me, I refocus on the knife. It isn't right. I need Dad's skinning blade.

Phil retreats into the house as I stomp up the steps. I storm through the kitchen, into the hunting room, and over to the cabinet where Dad keeps his knives. The top drawer scrapes as I pull it open. The stiff hinges of the metal box squeal as my fingers push back the dented lid. Again my hands drag down the front of Dad's jacket as I scan his razor-sharp knives laid out in a careful line, all in protective sheaths. My hand reaches for the stainless steel skinning blade.

"What do you think you're going to do with that?"

I ignore Phil and take the knife through the kitchen. She steps out of my way.

Back beside the rabbit, I sense Phil at the kitchen door. It takes all of my willpower not to glance back at her. Is she angry? Or does she feel sorry for me? Which is worse?

When Dad skins and guts game, he takes his time, works his knife over a carcass as smoothly as if he's pulling a blade through warm butter. He preserves every usable part of the animal. But my movements are clumsy and choppy. My hands shake as I drag the knife blade up the underside of the rabbit in a way that's too rushed. Sure, I've dissected dead squirrels and groundhogs before, but I didn't shoot them. And, yes, Dad has taught me all about dressing small game, but he never warned me that slicing the flesh of something I'd once seen alive would make me this squirmy.

Not once did he mention how warm blood could turn me queasy.

After I skin the rabbit, the raw and sticky body looks like something run over by a lawn mower. The air is heavy with the metallic odor of blood and guts. I shudder, feel as skinless and as hollow as the carcass.

The back door opens as I wipe my bloody hands through the prickly, strawlike December grass. Philly steps outside holding two long and thin boxes. She places the wax paper and aluminum foil on the stoop, where I can grab them.

I dip my chin in a silent *thanks.*

But she doesn't leave.

"It must have been hard to kill that rabbit," she says in a soft voice.

My hands fumble with the boxes. I rip off a piece of wax paper. "I'll get used to it."

"At least you're not trying to convince me that the kill came easy to you." She turns back to the door and pulls it open.

I glance up at her.

Holding the door ajar, she looks over her shoulder at me. "Since shooting that rabbit has already been tough on you, I won't tell Dad that you went hunting on your own."

"You're my hero," I mutter. "But I'm going to tell him about this rabbit as soon as he gets home."

Both of her eyebrows lift. "You're brave, for a twerp. Maybe too brave."

I wrap the rabbit meat in wax paper and then foil. Inside the house again, my thudding steps go straight to the freezer. I fling open the door and hurl the parcel onto an icy shelf.

"I hope I don't have to point out that there will be snow skiing in hell before I cook that."

Typical Phil: She'll eat the rabbit and deer meat that Dad brings home (she loves the venison jerky that he makes), but she doesn't want to know about it until it is cooked and camouflaged in vegetables.

"I hope I don't have to point out that I don't care what you cook."

The phone rings before Phil can come back at me with some snappy remark.

Phil goes for it. "Hello? . . . Hey, Tommy. Joey's right . . ." She stares at nothing, listening. "Uh, I'm fine." Phil twists her face, probably confused by Jacks's interest. Most of my friends give their toenails more attention than they give her.

"Hold on," she says while returning to the kitchen. "It's Tommy Jackson," she whispers. "And he's acting bizarre."

"I'm not here."

Philly's eyes pop as if I've just magically sprouted antlers. Probably because I've never turned away from any of my buddies before. Especially not Jacks.

Whatever. I drop the skinning knife to the counter and wrench the faucets to full blast. All I care about is getting the blood off of me. Once this happens, though, it's not enough. I grab the plastic bottle of dishwashing soap and pour enough orange goop over my hands to scrub most of Philadelphia clean.

"Joey is busy right now," Phil says into the phone. "Can I give him a message?"

Out of the corner of my eye, I watch her listen. Jacks is probably telling her that I missed another hockey practice. Maybe he's adding that I've been letting down my teammates. When Phil grinds her teeth, I'm pretty sure that he is mentioning the book report questions.

"Okay. I'll tell him to call you." But Philly doesn't hang up. Jacks, as smooth as sandpaper, must be jabbering on about hoping to see her around.

I'm still lathering my hands and scrubbing when Philly finally slams the phone into its base. "Tommy wants to know why you blew off hockey." She stares at me. "He said your coach went ballistic when he realized that you'd skipped another practice."

What am I supposed to say? That I'm a humongous loser for not showing up at the rink today, for killing an innocent rabbit?

"Tommy has your book report questions, Joey. He would have given them to you at hockey practice, if you'd shown up." Impatience soaks through her words. "Letting down your team is not cool."

"Coach knows that I'm good for the Jersey game," I snap. "He'll get over a couple missed practices."

Philly doesn't comment, which she probably thinks makes her big sister of the year. In two strides she's at my side, pulling me back from the sink. "Enough."

Staring at my hands, I blink. I sniff. I can't help it. But I refuse to glance at Phil as I shrug away from her. Instead, I step back to the sink, pick up the skinning knife from the counter, and plunge it under the faucet. The rabbit's blood runs off the blade, swirls pink.

Philly sighs. "Joey, I've never seen you this freaked out. What can I do?"

Once the water runs clear, I drop the knife back onto the counter. I grab a dish towel. Instead of drying the blade, I start dragging the cloth over my hands. Why can't I wipe away the gummy rabbit warmth?

Phil yanks the towel from me. "Keep scrubbing and you won't have any skin left."

I head for my room.

"Joey, wait. Listen." Philly stops at the kitchen doorway. "Concentrate on hockey and your drawing. Focus on what you love, Little Brother, on what you're good at."

"Butt out, Phil. BUTT OUT!" I claw my hearing aid from my ear and throw myself into my bedroom, slamming the door behind me. I drag my palms over my jeans as my sister's words ring in my ears. Even without the hearing aid.

CHAPTER 11

THREE DAYS LEFT

Hours come. Hours go. The red 11:26 on the face of the digital alarm clock glows. It's beyond weird that Dad is out this late on a Tuesday night. My hearing aid is back in my left ear. The minute he comes home, I'll tell him that I shot something with a heartbeat.

My back presses the pillows mashed against the headboard of my bed. Claude is curled at my feet, watching me. Accusations cloud his yellow eyes. I'm sure he knows about the rabbit.

My head feels like it has stopped a speeding puck. My stomach might be on fire. Mom would blame the five chocolate bars and two sodas I inhaled. But the head pounding and gut burn has more to do with that rabbit. Of course, the mess Philly called dinner isn't helping. Nice that she attempted my favorite meal, Mom's creamed chicken and mushroom crepes, but it was scary. My autopsy revealed pre-fried, frozen chicken fingers in canned mushroom soup instead of fresh chicken in Mom's cream sauce. And Philly wrapped her glop in frozen pancakes thawed in the toaster oven instead of making Mom's paper-thin crepes. I'd rather have had a bowl of cereal for dinner, but I couldn't do that to my sister. She thinks she's a decent cook.

Despite my insides, I draw on the only sketch pad that I can find. The others must be lost under clothing, hockey padding, comic books, and empty bags of Cheez Doodles and jerky. One of these days I'll clean my room. Maybe.

But tonight the scratch of my pencils on paper doesn't settle me. The feel of the rabbit's body is still on my fingers. Even the smooth wood of the pencil isn't enough to replace this ick.

Shooting a rabbit has never been a big deal to Dad. Will it be now? Will this be enough to make him want to be hunting buddies with me again? Or will he give me thirty years to life for hunting on my own?

With these questions echoing between my ears, it is a miracle that sleep sneaks up on me. When it does, it brings nightmares about rabbits and gunshots and too much blood. Until the rumble of Dad's truck interrupts.

I launch off the bed. Claude goes flying. As I crack open the bedroom door, yellow light from my room spills into the dark and silent living room.

If I had two bum ears, I still would have heard the back door crash open, the slam of the kitchen table, the scrape of its feet across the tiles. "Useless piece of tin crap, pain in my—"

Dad? Why is his voice unstable? Why are his words fuzzy?

He rips into a string of blurry curses that I've never heard come out of his mouth. "This place is exactly what my life has become. A filthy hole." He slams the bottom of a beer onto the table.

Beer? Since when?

The slam knocks him off balance. He almost falls over. When he recovers, he flings a fist at nothing. Beer goes flying. Foam sprays the chairs that Mom painted white last summer. She'd pass out if she saw this. But then, if she was here, Dad wouldn't be throwing punches.

There's no way Philly is sleeping through this, but her bedroom door stays shut. I'd give away my best comic books to have her come out and back me up.

Anger twists Dad's face, turns him gargoyle ugly. "Of course she's taken off again for God knows how long," Dad spits. "You're a useless husband and father."

Reason number two hundred and one why I'm hating those stupid Zuckermans. A kid shouldn't feel sorry for his dad. This is as wrong as wrong gets.

This is Mom's fault.

I cross the living room, slow. As I hit the light from the kitchen, Dad turns to me. He squints to make me out.

"Hey, Dad. Are you all right?" I try to sound cool, casual.

"Do I look *all right*?" His tone challenges.

I shot a rabbit clumps in my throat.

"You deaf? I asked you a question."

He might as well have backhanded me. I fight the urge to yank the hearing aid out of my ear and bolt back to the safety of my room. "No, sir, not deaf."

He staggers toward me. Unsteady. And not just because of his limp. Stale cigarette smoke clings to him, mixes with the bite of beer. "Or maybe you're like me, got your head stuck up your butt."

I suck in a breath, back off. Dad has always taught Philly and me that the stronger person walks away from a confrontation.

"Where did I mess up?" His right shoulder hits the doorway that connects the living room to the kitchen. He falls back. "What do you want from me?"

"I don't want anything." This isn't true. I want him to stop being mad. I want him to laugh again and tell his bad jokes. I want him to smile and watch Philly and me when he thinks we don't know it with a look that says we've done something amazing when we haven't. I want him to stay up late to read some history book or magazine, not to drink beer at the Hunter's Inn. I need him to smell of Mom's favorite cologne, not cigarette smoke.

His head jerks as if I've smacked him. His eyes narrow. "You using a tone with me?"

"No, sir."

He turns away. "Useless," he hisses, the word thick and slimy.

Useless?

He turns back around. "You know what I had to do all night?" His glare punctures.

"No, sir," I choke out. Why doesn't Philly get out here?

"I had to listen to Sam Hector brag about how his son shot a deer." Dad's face tightens. "That kid pulled the trigger, no problem. But you get a buck in front of your nose and do nothing." Dad tilts his face to the ceiling. He clenches his mitt hands. "Stinking Sam did a better job teaching his kid to hunt. I never would have bet on that." He shakes his head. "Useless."

There it is. Proof that he was counting on me.

"I shot a rabbit," I blurt out in a desperate offering.

He keeps staring at the ceiling. He doesn't register what I've said. Or he doesn't care. He turns his back to me, half stumbles, half limps to the aspirin cabinet.

I fly back to my room. The hearing aid is already out of my ear.

Useless.

The nightmares come easy. Seven rabbits cluster around the one that I shot. Fourteen eyes full of loss. Their noses keep twitching the same silent question: *Why?*

And then comes the shake.

"Joey!"

Phil is doing her best to rattle my bones loose. "JOEY! Wake up! You're late!"

I sit up, push my bangs off of my face, expecting the rabbits to be staring at me.

"It's after seven!" Phil stands over me with her hands on her hips.

Wednesday. Nine days left of deer season. Three afternoons left before Saturday, three afternoons to prove that I'm not useless. "CRAP!" I cram my hearing aid in my ear. "Why didn't you wake me up earlier?"

"I'm not your keeper." She grabs a long-sleeved T-shirt off the floor, rolls it into a ball, and sidearm throws it at me. Jeans follow. "I thought you were in here doing homework. I should have known better."

"Homework. Double crap," I mutter.

Phil goes still. "Tell me you did your homework, Joey."

My eyes pick out the top of my still-zipped backpack under a muddied sweatshirt.

"Answer me, Joey. You did your homework, right?"

"Butt out. You're not Mom." I crawl out of bed, trying not to look at my sister.

She picks my latest sketch off the floor. Cartoon rabbits all over the page are running, jumping, grooming, and chewing dandelions. Their extra-long ears are tangled. Their tails are mashed against one another's. Their larger-than-life eyes glisten with sweet innocence.

She turns to my dresser and drops this drawing there.

And then she digs out another sketch pad from underneath a pile of comic books. She lifts the cover, scans the charcoal pencil portrait of Claude. Her fingers flip pages. Her eyes check out my sketches of rabbits, raccoons, squirrels, and Old Buck. Philly turns the drawings on their sides to study them at different angles. She flips back to Claude and studies this drawing upside down. I don't ask why.

"These are great, Joey. I almost expect them to breathe." The sketch pad slides off of Philly's fingertips, back onto the dresser. "But if you're failing your classes again, you can say *adios* to drawing time. Mom and Dad will fill your hours with nothing but tutoring. You'll be lucky to get a bathroom break. Once school ends, it'll be summer school." She turns on the toes of her sneakers and exits.

I leap out off my mattress, pull on the jeans and the T-shirt. As I grab a sweatshirt from under the bed, I hear the tapping on the window glass and roof. Icy flakes are dropping from a thick and gray, low-hanging sky. "Great," I snarl to no one. Once I find two more sweatshirts, I'm out of the room with my backpack.

The hockey posse minus Junior, as usual, walks slow, crunching and slip-sliding on the frozen glaze over the sidewalk leading up to the brick school. I'm the one who usually sets the pace and I'm dragging my sneakers. Most days people don't pass us, but today they do. They throw cheerful morning greetings, but I don't answer. Wet flakes land on my face and hands. But I don't care. I just burrow deeper into my sweatshirts.

"Tags, get it in gear," Jacks prods. "My grandmother and her walker move faster."

Useless.

"We're gonna be late," Katz mutters.

"And Tags, when are you going to share whatever lame excuse you have for missing practice yesterday?" Jacks glares over his shoulder at me. His tone is challenging.

I shrug.

The frown lines in his forehead go deeper. "What's with you?"

"Stuff."

Katz stops chomping on an apple and straightens out of his usual shoulder slouch. Cheets glances at me, his face finally registering that I wouldn't skip practices without a solid reason. The wrinkles in Jacks's forehead disappear.

"I shot a rabbit," I blurt out. My tone makes it clear that I hate what I've done. Especially since the rabbit wasn't good enough.

A minute ticks past. School buses rumble into the Jefferson Middle School parking lot, tainting the air with exhaust.

"That's more than I've shot," Cheets says.

"A rabbit?" Jacks's eyes go wide. "I thought you were going for a deer."

"I tracked some." My throat closes in on itself. "I had a

buck lined up." I fidget. "Have you ever looked into their eyes? You can see their fear."

Jacks focuses on the way his boots are crunching ice. My sneakers keep slipping. The snowflakes keep tapping. He shrugs. "I couldn't shoot a deer."

"Me neither," Katz mumbles.

I don't need to tell these guys how much I appreciate them saying this.

"Still, you deserve a beating for missing another practice," Katz adds. He punches my right arm, but he hops out of range before I can hit him back. As he glances at his watch, his shoulders droop again. "Come on. We're gonna be late." He inhales the rest of the apple.

Stepping into the warmth and chaos of Jefferson Middle School with the hockey posse helps me to leave the rabbit, the deer, and Dad's bet in the snow.

Cheets cuts left to go to his locker. Katz darts right. Jacks and I keep moving down the main hall. Just as the day seems doable, Junior busts into the building.

"Hey, Tags, Jacks. What's up?" He grins big as he catches up to us.

"Not much," I reply.

"How's life with a mouthful of train tracks, Jacks?" Junior laughs and snorts as if this is the funniest thing he's ever said. "Been hunting again, Tags? Shoot any baby birds yet?"

Jacks slaps my back. "Better. My man Tags shot a huge rabbit."

Just my luck that Jacks would bring this up.

"A rabbit?" Junior's eyebrows spike. "That's all?" His hand pushes my arm. "You're kidding, right? Your old man tells everyone that you can track any deer anytime, but you only shoot a rabbit? No way." His laugh erupts in wet snorts. "That's hysterical."

I stomp off toward social studies, hoping I can lose him in the hall traffic. My hands go to my jeans and start wiping. Jacks follows me.

"A rabbit," Junior continues, coming after us. "The cats get all the mice?"

I turn to him. The crowd splits and flows around us. He's begging for a punch to the mouth to shut him up. I can almost taste the satisfaction that this would bring. It might be worth a suspension. But his happy expression tells me that he's clueless about how he's irritating me.

"Cram it, Junior," Jacks warns. "Tags wanted that rabbit. Everyone knows he can track and shoot a deer anytime. He knows how to find that buck that all the hunters talk about."

Junior jerks, sobers. "What? Old Buck?" He snorts. "Yeah, right."

I pivot and walk away.

Until Junior clamps one of his paws onto my arm and turns me to him. His expression tightens. His eyes give away his anxiousness. "You can find Old Buck? Really?"

I jerk my arm from his grip. "I might know where he hangs out." I move on.

"Tags, wait!" Junior scrambles after me, moves close to my good ear. "Listen, my dad's been all over me to help him nail that deer." Chuck's breath is the worst kind of skunk. "How about a deal? I'll get my old man to can the bet with your dad if you'll lead me to Old Buck."

My insides go cold. "No." I walk away from him. Again. Jacks follows.

"At least tell me where you've seen that buck. Give me a clue, man. What do you care?" He lumbers after me.

No response.

He stops. "You know what? I don't think you can track crap, MacTagert. If you could, you'd prove it. You'd have shot more than a stupid rabbit by now."

"Lighten up, Junior," Jacks snarls over his shoulder.

I'm speed-walking, but I glance back at the kid. He's deflated. He's lost his bravado. Something flickers in his round, dark eyes. Fear?

Jacks watches me watching Junior. "Don't worry about him. Let him find his own deer."

But Junior's expression is scratching at me. "Sometimes that kid acts like he's scared."

Jacks shrugs. "He just wants to shoot a big antlered deer for his dad."

"To win the bet."

"Nah." Jacks waves this away with one hand. "If the bet was important, Junior wouldn't shut up about it. No one but you thinks it's a big deal, Tags."

I grunt instead of arguing.

"Forget about Junior. Concentrate on getting your butt to hockey practice this afternoon."

I'm only half listening. Because the only way to erase *useless* is to bring home Old Buck.

First period is a nuclear meltdown. When I come up with nothing to turn in for homework, McDrab calls me to his desk.

"Yes, sir?" I use my most polite tone. I act as if I have no clue why we're about to have one of those teacher-student chats where the teacher does most of the talking.

He studies me over the top of his glasses. "Are you aware, Mr. MacTagert, that you are dangerously close to failing my class?"

I shake my head no. Right now I'm more aware of the mentholated cough-drop odor coming off of him. It's hitting me full on, making me dizzy, and setting my sinuses on fire.

"I suggest you make up the homework assignments that you've missed by the end of the week." He sounds bored, but he taps the pile of turned-in homework with the eraser of his pencil.

"Yes, sir. I will. No problem." And I actually sound like I mean it.

By the time second-period Spanish is over, I've made my decision.

• • •

For once, having my locker at the back of the school works out well. No one sees me here. No one asks where I'm going or why I'm not in a class.

"Better get your caboose in gear, sugar." Mrs. Fritz, head lunch lady, shuffles past me carrying a dented, industrial-size, metal baking pan. Her perfume is oil of French fries. A spider's web hairnet lies over her graying, frizzy hair. Most of the cafeteria people peel these off when they leave the kitchen. Not Fritzy. "I'd hate to see you be late for class and get written up." She smiles, her teeth crooked but her eyes shining. She's a big woman with an even bigger heart.

"Never happen," I joke as my fingers pause on the dial of my combination lock. I flash her a grin. "See ya later, Mrs. F!"

"If I'm lucky," she says. And then she disappears down the hall.

I wait for the feeling of being watched to leave me. But it doesn't. The price of skipping school.

I give the locker door a yank. It sticks before it opens with a clang and too many rattles. Typical. Piece of crap. I grab a book in the name of homework, close the locker door, and then bolt, telling myself that my twitching nerves are stupid. "Fritzy's in the halls. That's all." I slam into the panic bar on the back door, the one with the alarm always off.

Cold smacks me in the face. Instead of tasting like sweet freedom, it has the bitter flavor of fear.

CHAPTER 12

WEDNESDAY AFTERNOON

The shiny red truck that belongs to the Cheetavera family is parked on the grassy shoulder of Mill Road, right across from the opening to the clearing in front of Dewey's woods. It's my kind of luck that Cheets's father, one of the two hunters other than Dad allowed on Mr. Dewey's land, would be here. As if my having to track down and shoot Old Buck isn't hard enough, now I have to avoid being seen.

There's zero time to worry about this, though. I've already lost time stopping home to get my hunting gear. So I push fast through the field grasses.

Halfway across the clearing, a dark-haired guy about Dad's age, but shorter than him, emerges from the trees. In his bright orange cap, vest, and camouflage jacket, he could be on the cover of one of Dad's hunting magazines. This grown-up version of Cheets, a man with the same dark, round eyes and globe face, is moving quick and lugging a rifle in one hand.

"Joey?" His deep voice is urgent in a way that I'm not used to. His eyebrows arch and his eyes swell. He takes longer strides toward me, which makes me nervous.

"Hey, Mr. Cheetavera." My voice cracks. My cardboard smile wobbles.

"Joey, what are you doing here?" No smile. His face is pale under a sheen of sweat. He scans my hunting gear. His eyes linger on Granddad's gun for twenty seconds that feel like two hours. And then his serious eyes find mine. "Joey, you're not allowed to hunt on your own."

Think fast! "Yes, sir, I know." My mind puts together an acceptable reason for me to be here with a gun. "I'm, uh, waiting for my dad." Of course! "He's meeting me here." I force a smile.

Mr. Cheetavera shakes his head. "Don't go into those woods, Joey. A couple of hunters are poaching in there. One of them has been drinking. They have traps." He shakes his head again. "No telling how many they've already set."

His alarm pushes me back a step. A foot caught in a trap can mean one less foot.

"I'm heading to John Dewey's place to call the police." Cheets's dad holds up a small, silver cell phone with his free hand. "I can't get a signal out here." He marches past me, heading for Mill Road. "Come on. I'll give you a ride back to your house."

"Thanks," I say, thinking fast again, which is some kind of record for me. "But my dad is on his way here. I'll wait for him, tell him what you said so that he doesn't go into those woods, either." Wow, I'm good.

Mr. Cheets hesitates, studies me from over his shoulder.

I paste on what I hope is an innocent grin. "How about if I wait for him by Mill Road?"

"Okay." He marches toward the road again. I follow him. "But if your dad doesn't show up soon, you walk home. You hear me?"

"Yes, sir, loud and clear." At the opening of the meadow, I plop myself down.

Mr. Cheets flashes me a quick, but weak and worried, smile before he throws himself, his gun, and his cell phone inside the cab of his red truck. As he turns the engine over, he glances at me one more time. I whistle and pull at grasses, hoping my body language says, *I'm just sitting here, waiting for my dad.*

The truck hops off the shoulder and takes off. Once the engine grind fades, I sprint toward the trees. A fresh urgency is pumping through my veins, fueled by lost time.

At the tree shadows, I hesitate. Who else is in these woods? It doesn't matter. *You can do this,* I tell myself, using the words Coach says to me when the team needs me to score.

• • •

Dad's blind sits smack in front of me, waiting. It will have to keep waiting. To get a shot at Old Buck, I've got to track him. I've got to be on the move.

Worrying about Old Buck and who else is among these trees while scoping out each inch in front of me for hidden shark-toothed traps make my steps heavy and hesitant. It doesn't help that Granddad's rifle feels colder and more awkward than ever before. But none of this matters. "The rabbit wasn't good enough," I tell the trees. "I have to do this."

I push deeper into the forest. I'm already close to frozen, but at least the feeling of being tracked has faded. The footsteps that I thought I had heard padding after me almost all the way home from school evaporated near the Buckner place. At the same time as strains of violin music squeezed out through the sealed windows of that house.

Since then, my ears have not picked up on a scuff or a twig snap. But I'm still getting danger signal twinges that vibrate deep in my gut. Something is not right.

It's not long before my nose picks up new moist wood. This scent leads me to gouged streaks of raw yellow tree pulp more than a few feet up on a thick oak. Fresh antler scrapes.

My heart starts to hammer. My hand snakes under the orange hunting vest and into Dad's coat pocket, searching for cartridges. Along the way, my fingers brush Mrs. D's credit-card-size digital camera. Someday I'll remember to give it back to her.

"Focus," I say out loud.

I pull the rod out from the front of the rifle, drop a cartridge into the magazine, and then slide the rod back in. My shaking hands do this five more times for five more cartridges, five more shots. Next, I pull the lever under the rifle back to chamber a round. My breath catches in my throat as the cartridge clicks into the barrel, making the gun ready to fire. Only my easing the hammer forward slows the gallop of my heart.

With Granddad's gun locked and loaded, I take slow steps. No cracking branches. No crunching leaves. The compass needle in my gut points a firm right. I turn that way. My nose fills with the smell of musty, decaying leaves along with the wet and mineral tang of mud. And a sweet muskiness. Deer, dead-on ahead of me.

I head toward the stream until a twig snaps about fifty feet behind me.

I freeze.

Shriveled leaves rattle without a breeze.

I crouch, scan my surroundings the way Dad has taught me to do. "Squirrels," I whisper when I hear nothing more. But I'm not convinced.

I move again, slow. The air almost vibrates with a sense of danger. "Real hunters don't get freaked," I tell myself. "Focus on the fresh hoofprints pressed into the stream bank." This is what Dad would do. The prints point at the water. So does my compass needle.

Dad's voice pounds in my head: *Never cross a fence or barrier without disarming your weapon.* Right. I pull the rifle lever six times to eject the six cartridges. I pick them off the ground and slide them into my jacket pocket. Somewhere behind me, leaves shuffle and crunch. My hands tighten on the gun. "I'll use it as a club if I have to," I mutter. And then I step on stones to cross the stream. Dad's boots slip. My feet slide. It's a miracle that I don't wipe out.

On the opposite side of the stream, I head for the cluster of white-skin birches that stand at the edge of the clearing with the stone wall. The place where I disappointed Dad. In a repeat of last Saturday, my sixth sense is right on. A big buck with an impressive rack of antlers stands at the far side of the clearing. He'd make a nice drawing, the way he's pulling at tufts of grass with his teeth and chewing. The furless scar across his face confirms what I already know.

Hello, Old Buck.

Score, I guess.

He lifts his head to check me out. His big ears flick forward and back. Does he recognize me as the kid with the pencils and the paper? Does he expect me to sit and draw him again or take his picture with Mrs. D's camera? *I'm hauling more than pencils and a camera today,* I want to warn him. If he only knew that he's my best chance to make Dad proud.

I force my hands to reload the rifle. I fumble with the cartridges. My breathing is choppy and ragged. My hand pulls the lever under the rifle to make a cartridge slide into the barrel. Old Buck doesn't even flinch.

I move slowly toward him, shifting the butt of the gun to my shoulder. My eye lines up with the sights on the barrel. Adjusting it to point at my deer's heart is about the hardest thing that I've ever done. "Aim and fire," I whisper, repeating Dad's words. They stick in my throat. My eyes burn. "Hunters don't cry," I remind myself.

I gut the doe . . . steaming blood and guts are everywhere . . ., Junior had said with zero regret.

I force my trembling pointer finger around the trigger.

Squeeze the trigger. NOW!

Seconds drag into minutes as I imagine the thumping of Old Buck's heart under his fur, the flow of his blood within the plumbing of his veins, where it belongs. His steam breath looks like tufts of cotton as it leaves his nostrils. His eyes flicker with a child's curiosity.

I can't. I *can't* fire at him! The way I could never shoot at Claude or at Winston. This certainty rolls over me with the weight and power of a speeding eighteen-wheel truck.

But there is no time to dwell on it. Sticks snap no more than thirty feet behind me. Brush crackles. My fingers go to my hearing aid to turn up the volume.

A gunshot cracks. The bang is close enough to me to make me wonder if I've fired Granddad's gun.

"I got him! A buck!" This yell that bounces off of the trees belongs to the last person I want to see. Sam Hector.

I turn right and then left, searching. Where is Old Buck? Has he taken a bullet?

His white flag tail is up and on the move. There's no red splatter on his gray-brown coat as he leaps into tree shadows. My heart leaps with him. Score in overtime!

"I got him," Sam announces again from about twenty feet behind me. His boots plow through ground cover, heading my way.

Dad would tell me to yell to alert him that there's another hunter nearby, meaning me. But something tells me that this isn't news to Sam. Something tells me to take off. I do.

Before I can stumble all the way across the clearing, birch branches snap and break as if a gorilla is plowing through those trees. I look back over my shoulder. Sam stands swaying at the edge of the meadow. His cold, red-rimmed eyes narrow on me. He's gripping his shotgun in one hand, clutching a beer can in his other mitt.

I stop. Is this the guy Cheets's dad had discovered?

"You don't look like a buck full of shot to me, boy." He spits a wad off to his left. "What'd you do with my deer?"

When I don't answer right away, he drops the beer can and lifts the wavering shotgun. He aims the barrel at me the way I had aimed Granddad's gun at Old Buck. "Wait, maybe you are the deer." And then he laughs.

I imagine being sprayed with buckshot pellets.

But then Junior, hauling three rattling, rusty, sharp-toothed traps, slides up behind his father. Needle pricks ladder-climb up my backbone. Did Junior see me leave school? Did he follow me? Did he lead his dad here?

A black flashlight the size of Junior's forearm hangs from his belt. For spotlighting. All at once I want to slam him with everything I've got. Only Sam's shotgun keeps me back.

"Dad, that's Joey MacTagert," Junior says low.

"Junior, what are you doing here?" The question falls out of my mouth. I almost add that he should be in school.

He stares at the ground, where my gun barrel is pointed.

I glance at his dad, and then back at Junior. My mouth falls open. "Did you—" I swallow hard, unable to believe what I have to ask. "Did you follow me out of school? Did you and your dad wait for me to lead you to Old Buck?" This can't be possible. Junior's a member of the hockey posse. Buddies don't set each other up.

"Bang!" Sam's voice explodes, almost as startling as a real gunshot. His rifle jerks, still pointed at my chest. Beer slops over his hand.

I almost fall over, sure that I am history.

When I realize, after a couple seconds, that I'm not dead, I straighten. I stand tough, knowing one thing for certain: There's no way that I'm going to let this rock-head think that I'm scared of him.

"Dad!" Junior stares at his father. "Dad," he repeats, this time pleading.

Sam throws his huge head back and laughs. This, or what he's been drinking, makes him stagger backward. The shotgun barrel drops, points at the ground. More beer spills as Sam's back slams a birch. His laughter turns into a curse. He spits and then narrows his bloodshot eyes on me. "Old Buck belongs to us. He's my trophy. You hear me?"

"Old Buck doesn't belong to anyone," I answer, slow and defiant.

Sam's top lip rolls up in a snarl. He lifts the gun barrel, points it right at me. I stare into the black of its hollow center.

Junior grabs his arm. "Forget him, Dad. Come on. Let's go after Old Buck."

Sam glares at me, poised to squash me. Or shoot me. Or both.

"If I see you near that buck again—" He steps toward me. The shotgun wavers. "If I see you near that buck, this gun might go off." Sam stares right at me, spits a wad. "Get it?"

"Forget about Joey MacTagert, Dad." Junior keeps tugging on his father's arm. "Let's go blow away Old Buck. Then you can mount his head. Everyone will see that you're still the best hunter around."

Sam makes eye contact with his son. For a blink, there is appreciation in the man's face. He picks up his beer can and then he lets Junior lead him across the clearing, toward my deer.

"Kiss Old Buck good-bye," Sam calls back at me.

I pull out Mrs. D's camera. I'm not sure why except that I want proof that Sam and Junior were here. The LCD screen frames Sam with his beer and shotgun. It shows Junior leading him. And hauling traps. My fingers click off a couple fast shots.

Seconds after the last camera click, Junior and his father discover the deer path that is Old Buck's escape route.

"Get ready to blow that buck away, boy." Sam belly laughs as he and Junior disappear between scrubby pines.

This cannot be the way that Old Buck goes down. Not from two dirtbags that I've led here. I can't let this happen.

CHAPTER 13

THE FIFTH DAY OF ANTLERED DEER SEASON, CONTINUED

Every nerve in my body is telling me that I need to get out of these woods. Still, I keep on tracking the Hectors. I refuse to let them shoot Old Buck even though Sam is wasted and seems to be okay about blowing my head off. And he'd get away with it out here. Who'd turn him in? Not Junior. Yeah, I can almost hear the Hectors blaming everything on M. K. Buckner.

Here it is, the fifth day of antlered deer season and instead of trying to make myself shoot a deer, I'm risking everything to save one. But at least this feels right. Finally. I'll just have to figure out how to explain this to Dad.

Crushed branches and crumpled underbrush along the deer path, along with the sour stench of beer and body odors, mark the Hectors' trail. The curses and the clanking traps confirm that I'm heading in the right direction.

"Hurry up, jackass," Sam yells at Junior.

Again, I feel kind of sorry for the kid, now that I know how insults from a dad feel.

But I hang back, far enough to see these two without being seen. Breathing in soft bursts that I hope are soundless, I pick my steps carefully, pause often to listen. My head pounds with the same question: How can I keep the Hectors from getting to Old Buck?

"Where'd that deer go?" Sam growls. "We can't lose him. If we stay with him until it gets dark, we can spotlight him."

My stomach clenches. Blinded, Old Buck won't have a chance. "Losers," I mumble. And I move too fast. Leaves stir.

Junior stops. "I heard something behind us."

I go still.

Sam belches.

I hold my breath.

"Maybe it's the buck," Sam decides. A loud shotgun cracks. The blast echoes out, spreads in rings.

"I got'm that time! Old Buck!" Sam lets out a whoop that sends my heart into the toes of Dad's boots.

"You shot at something *behind* us," Junior says. He sounds worried. "Old Buck is in front of us. Remember?"

"Shut your hole and follow me. I'll show you what I heard." Sam tears through brush, heading right for me. "And if I catch anyone near my deer, he'll be real sorry."

I cut and run, tear back to the clearing as fast as possible. Dad's boat boots might as well be cement blocks. Granddad's gun might as well be an anchor. Already I've figured out that trying to get away was the most stupid thing that I could have done. As if Sam coming after me isn't bad enough, there is no time to scan for hidden, razor-toothed traps.

"It's Joey MacTagert," Junior yells. "Not a deer! Don't shoot him, Dad! Don't!"

Sam is tearing after me. "Shut up. I know a deer when I hear it."

I rip through brush, bounce off trees, stumble over rocks, sucking down gulps of air. Thorns claw at my jeans. Branches and vines whip my face. My heart hammers. Now I know how a deer feels during hunting season.

Sam hurls furious curses.

"Joey!" Junior yells, also running now. "Stop! Please!"

I keep running. At least I'm leading them away from Old Buck.

But they're gaining on me.

At the clearing, I spot the crumbling old wall where I've sat to draw Old Buck. Do I have enough time to get to this hiding place before Sam reaches the meadow? As I push for it, Dad's voice echoes in my ears. *Never cross a fence or barrier without disarming your weapon. Unload it.* But there's no time. I can't stop.

I shift Granddad's rifle to my left hand. My right palm comes down hard on the wall. I launch my body up. It arches, turns, flies, with all my weight on the right arm. My legs swing up in a beautiful vault. I am almost home free.

Until a shot rings out.

It is sharp thunder that reverberates through me as if I'd swallowed a lightning bolt. My body drops, hits the wall, and bounces over it. What happened to my perfect vault? Why am I landing on my back, on a mattress of dried leaves? Why is my right foot on fire? And why does a fog of burned gunpowder hang over me?

I might throw up.

Boots gallop toward me.

"Oh, crap! Oh, man! Oh, crap, crap, crap!" Junior's thin face peers over the wall at me. His eyes are Ping-Pong balls. "Tags, man, your foot! OH, CRAP!"

It takes everything I've got to push with my forearms and lift my upper body, but I have to see what Junior's freaked about. Starting at my waist, I scan down my thighs, past my knees, and down my calves. As the thick, metallic stench of blood reaches my nose, my world spins. Whatever is in my stomach heaves. Because the toe of Dad's right boot has been torn open. Underneath the ripped leather, my foot is raw, bloodied meat.

NO! This can't be happening! My top half falls back onto the leaves again. My hands grab at my hair. No! No! NO! This can NOT be happening! Dad is going to kill me!

Sam's big head appears over the wall. His eyes take a couple seconds to focus. And then all the color drains from his skin. "Son of a—"

"What'll we do?" Junior squeals.

Sam turns away from me. His boots stomp off fast. Everything is becoming liquid. I am starting to sink.

"Dad? Where are you going?" Junior whines. "We can't leave him!"

"Get your carcass over here! NOW!" Sam's voice is farther off. "I'm not going to be blamed for this."

I try to sit up again. This can't be happening. "Junior," I croak. "Help me!"

He leans forward. The traps clank. His face twitches with an agony that looks like indecision. "Tags, man—"

"Yo, jerk-boy," Sam bellows. "What did I say? Get over here before I make ya sorry you were born!"

"I'll, I'll call someone, Tags." With a last tortured look that seems to say *I'm sorry,* he turns away from me. Leaves scatter as he runs off.

As the afternoon sun sinks behind the dense trees, I'm writhing, trying to find relief from the scalding knife slices centered in my foot and spreading through my entire body. Shadows slide over me as quickly as the reality that I'm alone and that I can't stand up and walk out of these woods to get help.

I shouldn't be here to begin with. No one but the Hectors knows that I'm behind this wall bleeding out from a blown-apart foot. *Scared* isn't a big enough word. My heart is racing out of control, but not from fear alone. My body is in overdrive. From my injury? From the pain? I don't know.

I can't think. I'm sinking again, spinning. I'm chilled, shaking and getting colder.

At least Old Buck is safe. For today. Or is he?

Someone far, far away calls my name. "Mom?" I need her. I'm going deep, deeper. "Help!" I choke out.

The voice calls again. But it doesn't belong to Mom. Philly? No, she's at cross-country practice.

Now something huge is plowing through the woods, coming at me. I squirm, twist. My foot screams in protest. I almost cry out, but I don't, afraid of what is heading my way.

The thing gets closer. When the trampling of brush and shattering of branches reaches the edge of the meadow, I squeeze my eyes closed. I don't know what else to do.

Crashing footsteps cross the meadow. I think I hear heavy breathing and then a low growl. The steps stop on the other side of the wall. I sense an immense presence leaning over it, peering down at me. When I crack my eyes open, a huge shadow jerks back. It grunts, leans down. Warm breath falls onto my face. It has the sugared, candied scent of bubble gum, mixed with the ingrained taint of cigarettes.

A pitiful yelp that should be a scream comes up from my throat.

"Stay calm," says a low, deep voice. The words swirl in my head.

The shadow straightens and jumps over the stone wall, dropping to his knees and bending over my foot. Even through my haze, I see salt-and-pepper buzz-cut hair and a black bandana twisted into a rope that is tied around a big, square head. I think I see a choker of beads around a thick neck.

I jerk in a desperate attempt to get away, but a big hand comes down on my thigh with gentle pressure. Something about this heavy touch is reassuring. Not that I could escape. The guy could decide to chew on my limb like a chicken leg and I couldn't do squat about it.

The reassurance doesn't last more than a beat, is interrupted by the metallic clanking of traps moving fast toward the wall. "Tags!" Junior's face appears over me. "I called 911 and—" He gasps. His mouth drops open. A whimper trickles out from his throat before he turns and bolts.

The big man hovering over me doesn't seem to care. Breathing loud and heavy and in short bursts, sometimes grunting, he is in a serious froth as he peels off his orange vest, olive-green canvas jacket, and then sheds a black hooded sweatshirt. One of his thick arms slides under my shoulders as his free hand wraps me in the sweatshirt. It reeks of tobacco. He arranges the hood up and around my head so that it falls partway over my eyes. Next, he puts the camouflage jacket around me. I'm swaddled, but still freezing.

Material rips. The big hands wrap something around my ankle and cinch it tight.

In the next instant, the huge arms scoop my body up,

off the leaves. I want to fight this, but I can't. I'm lifted high. And then the rocking starts. The man is running in long, loping strides. His breathing is hoarse, quick paced, and desperate. My head, as heavy as a bowling ball, bangs against his chest and his flannel shirt. But my carcass foot is held steady somehow. Is it still attached to my leg? All I feel is the throbbing and the burn. There is no sense of a foot.

"JOEY?" A high-pitched shriek shakes the treetops.

Through my haze and the breathing and the rocking, I recognize Philly's voice. But all I can do is moan.

My ride crashes over saplings and through sticker bushes. The way he dodges trees and the claws of their branches tells me that he knows these woods.

Not a whole lot of time goes by before I think I hear sirens wailing. And I think we're moving toward them.

Philly's three-note signature whistle, which comes from her shoving two fingers into her mouth and blowing, echoes out from behind me. One note comes out high, the next comes out lower, and the last blares an exclamation. This causes loud and excited voices to spring into action somewhere ahead.

"I thought I heard the whistle over that way," an unfamiliar male voice calls.

Sticks snap and crackle and brush gets mowed over by someone scrambling toward my ride and me. "Philly?" The voice is sure and reliable, but I'm not used to him sounding frantic.

I crack my eyes open when someone pulls back the hood.

Dad dashes at me. "Joey!" His arms shoot out, reaching. His eyes flash with wild fear.

"Dad," I manage to croak. I want to tell him that I messed up big-time. I want to tell him that I'm sorry, really sorry.

"My God, son—your foot. What happened?"

"The bullet went clean through," the low, rumbling, bubble-gum-scented voice says before I try to answer.

"Joey—" Dad sounds like he's in more pain than me.

The man slides me into Dad's open arms. "Thank you," my father says with trembling gratitude. He wraps his arms around me, pulls me close. All at once I'm safe and protected despite the pulsating pain at the end of my leg. I melt into Dad's chest, absorbing his warmth and his cologne with Mom's perfume twisted into it. The image of them together again calms me.

Dewey's meadow is washed in the bright, blinking red and blue lights of two police cars. Within a minute I'm surrounded by other people's panic. And uniforms. Static, nasal voices talk back and forth over car radios.

"You're going to be all right, son," Dad tells me in a soft, tender voice. But he doesn't sound certain. "Someone called 911. An ambulance is coming." For once, he speaks close to my bad ear. His hands lower me into the back of his Jeep, and prop my mangled foot up on old blankets. "Leave it there, Joey." He peels off his wool coat, lays it over me.

"Dad?" Philly's voice, sounding desperate and searching, calls from the edge of the woods.

"Philly!" Dad turns, ready to bolt, but he doesn't need to. She's already running toward us. He goes to her, wraps her in a tight hug. "Where have you been?" His voice is shaking. "Are you all right? What happened to your head?"

"I ran into a tree looking for Joey." She was out in those woods, in the dark, looking for me? Is she crazy? Did she hear Sam and Junior out there? Did she know how much danger she was stepping into? For me?

"Looking for Joey?" Dad's voice turns bold. "What is going on?"

Oh, no.

"Joey is out there hunting, trying to impress you," Phil screams. "But it's too dark. We need flashlights and—"

"Philly." Dad places his hands on her shoulders. "Joey is here." Dad points at me.

I try to lift my head. I want to say *Thanks, Phil.* For caring so much. Somehow I've been missing this.

"Joey!"

Dad lifts an arm, barricading her from diving into the back of the Jeep, on top of me. "Don't touch him."

She blinks and blinks again over bugged-out eyes that are filling with tears. "Is he dead?"

"No," Dad tells her, sounding worn out. He pulls in a heavy breath. "In shock, I think."

"What, what happened to his foot?" Phil's voice squeaks.

"He's going to be okay, Philly." Dad's trying to force a calm, cool tone.

"The Hectors," I croak. "Traps. Spotlighting."

"Shhh, son," Dad whispers, leaning down to me. His hand strokes my forehead. "You need to stay calm."

I relax a little under his touch. I think I hear one of the officers telling the radio something about two suspects.

"How did he get here?" Philly's voice almost gives out.

"He found Joey." Dad's voice is low and kind of amazed. He tips his head in the direction of the cop cars.

When both Dad and Philly turn to look, I shift my head a quarter turn to glimpse what they see, which throws my world into a spin. Dusk is settling onto the field, but I can still make out one officer yakking into a radio. A second is speaking to the huge guy with the buzz cut and the twisted black bandana. He won't stop kneading the hem of his orange vest. And he keeps turning his face to Dad's truck, straining his neck to see inside it.

Questions explode like firecrackers in my head. Is this the guy who hauled me out of the woods? Who is he? How did he find me?

When he senses me gawking at him, his hands quiet and he stares back. His complexion is milky, his eyes soft and glassy with what seems to be concern.

“I don’t understand,” Philly says. “Who called the police?”

“I don’t know. Mr. Cheetavera called me after he stopped by our house and found Joey wasn’t home,” Dad says. “He was worried that your brother had gone into the woods. I raced over here. He called the police. They told him that someone had called 911 and reported a shooting accident.”

I’m doing my best to absorb all of this when another siren screams in the distance.

“Please let that be the ambulance,” Dad mutters to no one in particular.

As if in answer, the siren gets louder. Bold bursts of light splash across Dewey’s meadow in a frantic, emergency rhythm.

The next thing I know, strangers are telling me that everything is going to be okay as they paw at me. Someone lifts one of my wrists and presses cool fingers into it. Sleeves are pushed up one of my arms. Velcro rips. Something is wrapped around my bicep. Unfamiliar voices are tossing medical terms and numbers back and forth. A needle pokes my forearm. It’s a mosquito bite compared with my burning foot and the dull ache within my chest. It’s all too much. My body gets heavier. I can’t fight the sinking anymore.

CHAPTER 14

AFTERWARD

I'm floating on fog. Or in a fog. Maybe I am the fog.

A thin tube is connected to my arm. I can feel the pinch of it. I can sense the plastic hose against my forearm. It must be attached to that bag of clear liquid hanging over my shoulder. The one I saw the last time I opened my eyes, when voices over me were talking about emergency surgery.

My nose is picking up sharp, antiseptic smells and starch from the crisp, folded sheets that I am sandwiched in between. A strange, bendable mattress supports me. My head and shoulders are raised, but I'm a long way from sitting up. This isn't my bed and I'm not at home.

A small voice deep inside my head suggests that I open my eyes. But this would take more energy than I have. Even with my eyes closed, though, I know that my right foot is a humongous, propped-up lump that doesn't feel a part of me anymore. It feels vague and ghostlike. I wiggle my right hand, my drawing hand. Thank goodness that it is solid and attached.

Soft fingers press my wrist. Cottony words brush my ears. Someone gentle is close, fussing with me and the assorted stuff that is around me. I think this person is a she. I'm certain I don't know her, yet her smell of plain soap and her clean breath are not new. "He's stable," she says to someone nearby.

Mom's favorite aftershave mixes with the thick roasted aroma of warm black coffee in a paper cup and the musky scent of a leather jacket. "Joey, I'm sorry." Dad's voice, low and close to my good ear.

"Go on," the soap-scented woman tells him. "He might hear you."

"It's an apology that's long overdue," Dad tells her, his voice heavy. "I lost my temper on our first hunt together. I don't know what came over me." He sighs. It's rippled with guilt. "Actually, I do know what came over me. But this is no excuse. And it sure didn't have anything to do with my son or hunting." A big, warm hand brushes over my forehead, pushes back through my overgrown hair to the crisp pillow supporting my head. I don't have to open my eyes to recognize the old dad. "And now he's shot himself in the foot."

What? My eyelids lift to half-mast. Dad, freshly showered, is dressed in ironed khaki pants, a button-down shirt, and his leather jacket, which he wears when he wants to look especially good. "What did you say, Dad?" My voice is croaky and rough and disbelieving.

"Joey." Relief washes over his shaved face. "You're back." His voice tells me that he's glad to see me and that I matter. But his smile disappears. His eyes glisten. His palm comes to the side of my face. "I'm sorry, buddy, but, yes, it seems that you shot yourself in the foot."

"*I* shot my foot?"

His face is my anchor as this information swirls around me. The nurse backs away from us. "What happened?" My question trickles out.

Dad blinks once, twice. "We were all hoping that you could tell us."

The details are starting to rise up where I can grab them. Me in the woods after I cut out of school. I found Old Buck. The Hectors found us.

"The camera?" I can barely hear my own question.

"Camera?" Dad sounds confused. "What camera?"

Mrs. D's camera. Where is it? Where are the pictures that I took of Junior and his old man? I remember Sam Hector coming after me. I remember running at the stone wall. "Granddad's gun," I push out.

"I've got it. Don't worry," Dad tells me.

I vaulted the wall. But did I unload Granddad's gun before doing that? I groan again.

"Joey?" Dad's eyes widen, the whites of them blaring.

I want to explain to him what I did, even if this makes

me more useless. But I'm spinning and dazed. "I don't think I unloaded Granddad's gun." I swallow. "Before the wall."

Dad stares at me for a stunned moment. I don't think he breathes. And then his pointer finger and thumb press into his eye sockets. "Oh, son." He lets out a long breath. It wavers. "What a horrible price to pay."

I don't know what to say. And I don't have the juice to say anything more anyway.

After many heavy heartbeats, Dad's hand moves to my arm and squeezes it gently. "I guess some lessons have to be learned the hard way." He rests his hand on his bum leg. "I ignored the rules of the road and of motorcycle riding once. I made a stupid mistake, too."

"Are you—" I hesitate a beat. "Are you disappointed in me?" The question seems distant, as if someone else has asked it.

"Disappointed? Joey, I hate that this has happened to you, but I'm not disappointed in you. I'm plenty disappointed with myself, but not you." He sighs. "In fact, I think I owe you an apology. After I gave up my motorcycle, hunting became even more of a passion for me. When you and I started going out into the woods together, tracking deer, I could see that you loved being out there as much as I did. I assumed that you'd love everything about hunting, that we'd share that. This was foolish of me."

"But I'm useless," I manage to mutter back.

"What?" He leans into me. He brings his other palm to the other side of my face so that he's holding my head in his hands. "Joey, why would you say that?"

I don't answer. My eyes close again. As long as I'm not useless, we're good.

"Is Joey awake?" Philly's voice fills the room as she busts into it. "Oh, he looks dead." Her voice cracks.

Dad's hands slide away from my face. "Philly," he says in a worn-out voice. "Your brother is far from dead."

"Far from it is right." The plain soap smell returns. "I can assure you that a dead body wouldn't be attached to bags of fluids, wouldn't be taking up our valuable hospital space, and wouldn't be hooked up to a monitor measuring a consistent heartbeat." The nurse fusses with something over my shoulder. "The bullet sliced an artery and crushed bone. Your brother lost too much blood and went into shock. His body needs to recuperate. The heavy sedation and medication will help with that, but he'll be dipping in and out of consciousness for a while."

Good to know. And I drift.

"But he's going to be okay, right?" Philly's question wobbles.

"He should be fine," Dad says. "He will need physical therapy to learn how to walk again, but losing a big toe isn't the end of the world."

Losing a what? I try to raise my eyelids, but a flush of coolness washes into my arm from the needle. The feeling spreads. A wave of calm floods me, mellows me without my permission.

"The important thing at this point is that he's stable—" The nurse's words get farther and farther away. "There's no infection."

One of us is fading. It might be me. I think I am sailing, swaying in a sturdy boat lined with starched sheets, my head on a thick pillow. I am gliding on a calm sea. After a while, I think I hear Mom singing "Twinkle, Twinkle, Little Star," her favorite lullaby, the one she sang to me most often. But she's far away, her voice is distant. "Mom?"

"I don't believe this," Dad says, close and muttering. "Your brother keeps asking for your mother. She's across an ocean and in a different time zone and I'm right here, but he keeps asking for her." A paper bag rustles. Tiny hard things clatter. Jelly beans. "I've screwed up, haven't I, Philly?"

This pulls me back, but my lips are too heavy to form words.

"Well, everything will be better when your mom gets here, which will be soon."

"It took long enough," Phil snaps. "Only thirty hours since Joey's surgery."

"It's not easy getting home from another continent," Dad says. "The airport closest to where she is doesn't have many flights out." Jelly beans clatter. "Don't blame your mother."

"Frankly, I'm blaming both of you." A sneaker tap-tap-taps the floor. The bed squeaks as Phil pushes up against it, leans into me. I can smell her floral shampoo and the goop that she puts on her hair when she styles it. "You better not have shot yourself in the foot on purpose, Little Brother," she whispers just for me. "To bring Mom home."

And then she leans back. "Has it occurred to anyone other than me that maybe Mom is needed by this family more than by a couple of rich geezers who take her to places with airports that don't have many flights out?"

The jelly beans stop rattling. "Yes, Philly," Dad says in a tight tone. "This has occurred to me. More than you know." He sighs. "Your mother and I have already talked about this. We need to talk more, and we will. But you also need to understand—" He stops. "We all need to understand that your mother loves her new job. She feels important and needed. You and Joey are not little kids anymore, you don't need her as much. There's no reason why we can't—"

I zone out. My parents back together and talking about serious stuff is enough.

"We'd better go," Dad adds. "I want to be at the airport when your mom's plane lands."

This explains his leather jacket, his ironed pants, and Mom's favorite aftershave.

Dad inhales another mile-long breath. "Philly, while I'm at the airport, could you please clean up the house, try to get it back into the shape that it was in before your mother left?"

"Like I haven't been doing all the cleaning, laundry, and cooking anyway?"

It's true. Philly really has been helping out more than anyone while Mom has been gone.

"I know, you've been great," Dad says. "But if you could just—"

"Consider it done," she tells him. "Mrs. Davies has already restocked the refrigerator with salad stuff." Philly's sneakers rubber-scuff over to him. "But if Mom is going to keep traveling, you, Joey, and me need to come up with a better routine. I need time to myself, space. I'm not doing all the cooking, the laundry, the cleaning, and whatever else anymore. I've got homework, track practices, and meets to deal with."

"You're right," Dad agrees before her rant builds momentum. "But for now, if the house is cleaned up, your mom might not figure out how badly things fell apart while she was away."

Phil lets go a sarcastic snort. "No, she won't have any idea."

I'd laugh if my sailboat wasn't floating away.

My nose fills with a clean linen scent that is not an undertone of Dad's cologne. Mom's perfume tugs me in off the gentle swells of a fog-covered sea.

"How could you let this happen?" Her question is a tear-soaked, restrained shriek. The shock waves of it ripple out through the room.

"He'll be all right," Philly whispers. But her voice wavers.

My eyelids flutter, as heavy as if someone placed a quarter on each. With effort, I open them enough to see Dad. He's beside my bed, kind of collapsed in on himself.

"I can't believe this," the tear-choked voice says.

"Mom, he's okay," Philly whispers in this strained but soothing tone.

Mom?

"Jill," Dad says. His voice is kind of pleading.

"I left you in charge and *this* happens?" Mom sniffs. Her hand touches my shoulder in soft, unsure taps.

"He won't break," Philly mutters.

"I left you in charge, Joe," Mom repeats to Dad.

Everything is hazy, swimming. I follow my nose and find the brown eyes and blond-streaked hair that I've been missing. "Mom," I croak. "You're the one who left." My eyelids, too heavy to hold up, fall closed again.

I'm not sure how much time passes before I return to the hospital room. This time, my head is clearer than when I last found the land of consciousness. I know the sweet scent beside the bed belongs to Mom. The cologne behind it goes with Dad. There's no more anger, no more blaming, so I open my eyes. My eyeballs are no longer wrapped in gauze.

Beside me, Dad's head pops up, his blue eyes wide, full of expectation. "Good morning." He smiles big.

"Hey, Worm," Philly puts in from behind him, through a bright grin.

"Morning," I croak out in my best frog.

"Joey, baby," Mom whispers from her place beside Dad.

I stare into her face, pale under faded makeup. I almost can't believe that she is close enough to touch.

"I'm sorry, honey." Her long fingers go to my forehead and comb my hair away from my eyes. Her gaze shifts to my bangs. Her lips part as she starts to say something, probably about my hair being too long, but she stops herself.

Dad places his hand on her shoulder.

She blinks quickly. "I'm sorry. You're right; I was the one who left."

"It's okay," I tell her.

Phil steps up beside Dad. "No, it's not." She folds her arms across her chest.

Dad's forehead bunches up as he turns to her. He sends her a warning look, special delivery. "Philly, this is not the time or the place for that discussion. Later, okay?"

Mom sniffs again. A tear skids down the left side of her face.

I'm about to say that I'm just glad that she is back, when bracelets tinkle near the doorway of my room. Mrs. D taps on the door. "Am I interrupting?"

"Joanne!" Mom goes to Mrs. D with open arms.

When Mrs. D breaks free from their hug, she scans faces. "Hello, Joe," she says. "Hi, Philly." She tries to smile. Her face doesn't seem willing. Her voice is soft and tentative until she sees that I am awake. "Joey!"

"Hey, Mrs. D."

She moves to the bed. Her quivering hand pats my upper arm. "How are you?"

"Your camera." I cringe as I pick the words to tell her. "I clicked off shots of poachers."

"You took pictures of the guys who followed you into the woods?" Her forehead lifts with her anxious question.

Mom turns to Dad. "What's this about people following him?"

"No one followed me," I say, still groggy. But then the truth of what happened slithers into the conscious part of my brain. But how does Mrs. D know that the Hectors followed me?

She leans toward me with bright eyes. "You took pictures of the Hectors poaching?"

"Yeah."

Mrs. D and Dad exchange quick glances.

"This could be the evidence that the police need." Dad pulls his cell phone from its holder on his belt. He punches buttons. "This could be what we need to defuse the rumors." He shifts the phone to his ear. "Excuse me," he says to us as he heads for the hallway.

"Joey," Mrs. D says. She pats my arm again. "How is your foot?"

"I'll be fine, no problem," I say, repeating what Mom and Dad told me.

"But how well he'll walk again depends on how his foot

heals," Phil adds. "If the shattered bones don't mend right, Joey might not be able to get around as well."

"What? No one told me that." I try to sit up, but Mom's hands go to my shoulders, guide me back down. "What about hockey?"

She looks straight into my eyes. I can see the sadness in the brown of hers. "Joey, honey, don't worry about any of that now. One day at a time." But her bottom lip is quivering.

Does she think my foot injury is going to affect my game? This has to be a nightmare that I'm going to wake up from.

"Everything will be fine, baby," Mom whispers.

Why has she stopped calling me "my man"? She only uses "baby" when things are bad.

I want to fire off more questions, but a tidal wave of emotions rolls into my throat.

And then Dad walks back into the room, the cell phone back on his belt. "Good news. Captain McHenry thinks the pictures Joey took could give the police what they need to put together a case against Sam Hector for poaching, trespassing, and illegal hunting."

"Dad—" I swallow hard. "I don't have the camera. I lost it."

He blinks, absorbing this. "Oh." He looks down. His enthusiasm slides off of his face. But then he comes over to me, places his hand on my shoulder. "Don't worry. Sam can't keep getting away with what he's been doing. He'll get caught breaking the law."

"Before Old Buck gets shot?" My voice cracks. My fear seeps out through that crack.

"Son, Sam hasn't taken down that deer yet. We would have heard if he had."

Mrs. D straightens and claps her hands together once. "Perhaps this is a good time to share some exciting news." She turns to me, inhales to the count of five. "Joey, as you know, I entered your drawing of the buck with the scar across his face in the Franklin Gallery Art Show."

"What?" I blink.

"Is this something else that I missed?" Mom sounds hurt.

Philly, still standing beside Dad, goes pale. She steps back slow, toward the door.

"Unfortunately, it turns out that participants have to be eighteen or older to exhibit work." Mrs. D shakes her head in slow disappointment.

"Wait," Dad interrupts. "I'm confused. What's this about an art show?"

Philly sighs. "Okay, I gave Mrs. Davies one of Joey's drawings to enter into an art show. And, okay, I did this without his permission." When everyone stares at her, she shrugs. "Joey is good at drawing. This art show was the perfect opportunity to show off his talent."

I turn to Dad. "I didn't know about this. I swear."

He pats my shoulder.

"Oh, dear," Mrs. D stammers. "I guess it's a good thing

that I didn't enter Joey's drawing, then, since he never gave his permission." She blinks at me. "I'm sorry."

"Me, too," Phil mutters.

"It's okay," I tell them. And I mean it.

"Anyway, while I was at the show," Mrs. D continues, "a gentleman who buys and sells animal drawings and paintings saw Joey's sketch." Fresh enthusiasm percolates into Mrs. D's face. "Joey, he wants to buy your drawing of Old Buck."

Mom and Dad go still, stare at Mrs D. So do I. But my sister leaps, yelping as if I had just scored the winning goal in a championship hockey game. "Ha! I knew it!" She punches the air the way she does when she wins a race. "I knew I was doing you a favor."

I blink. My anger and sadness get shoved aside for a moment by this news. And the fact that Philly has come through for me again. Sure, I should mutilate her for going into my stuff without asking, but I consider hugging her instead (even though I won't). "Someone wants to buy my drawing?" I blink, trying to absorb this. "Pay me money for it?"

"That's right." Mrs. D claps. "He suggested two hundred dollars."

My fingers go to my lame ear. Do I have my hearing aid in?

"I leave you people for a couple weeks and everything goes crazy," Mom is muttering.

The grin that flirts with Dad's mouth lets me know that I don't have to worry about the bear getting out of its cave.

"Two hundred dollars." He glances at me, looking kind of dazed and confused. "That must be some drawing. But Old Buck? How did you ever get close enough to—"

"I tracked him," I interrupt. "The way you taught me to."

He stares at me. "Oh, well," he stammers. "Wow. Well, that's, that's impressive."

"Congratulations, Joey," Philly says. "I guess it's time for you to start taking art more seriously." She glances at my bundled foot. "Especially since your future as a professional hockey stud is probably over."

My happiness is instantly zapped. Phil's words hit me with the force of a puck on the fly.

"You should be proud of your boy," Mrs. D says to my parents.

Instead of dismissing drawing as a hobby, Dad takes this in. He doesn't launch into a lecture about how hard it would be to make a living as an artist. Mom doesn't say squat about my time being better spent studying English, math, and science.

Dad kind of studies me, as if he's checking me out for the first time. As if my ability to sketch should be as obvious as a pencil-shaped birthmark. "You seem pretty thrilled about someone wanting to buy your drawing, son. I never realized that you pursued drawing with"—Dad rubs his forehead—"well, with such passion."

And that's when I realize what's been missing from my hunting. Passion.

Mom blinks at me. "How long have you felt this way about art?"

I shift under the sheets. I shrug. For a split second I consider denying ever having touched a pencil. But then I catch a glimpse of my wrapped foot and wonder how much of it is left underneath all the bandages, cotton, gauze, and whatever else. I stare at it until my hesitancy hardens into determination. I straighten as best as I can and lift my face to Mom and Dad. "Since forever." I nod. "Yeah, I've been loving drawing since forever."

Dad blinks at me. So does Mom. They blink at each other. They look as stunned as I feel. Where did this burst of confidence come from? Who knows, but I'm happy to have it.

"Loving drawing and art doesn't change him," Philly tells them. "He's still the same kid he's always been." She arches her eyebrows at Dad. "It's fine that he's not a duplicate of you."

Dad nods slow. "Yes, Philly, thank you."

"Joey's comic strips have always been impressive," Mom mumbles.

That's when Dad turns to Mrs. D. "Thank you, Joanne. This art business is welcome news after all that's happened." He pats his bad leg. "I know from experience that having something positive to hold on to goes a long way in helping a body heal."

Art is welcome news? Wow. Talk about something positive to hold on to.

"Spill it," Phil says in the no-nonsense tone that she uses to intimidate.

I will my eyes to open, but I stay sleep-still. Because watching Phil grill Jacks, Cheets, and Katz promises to be entertaining. And I could use a good laugh. The posse is lined up in front of her with their backs mashed against the wall across from the bottom of my hospital bed.

"Joey cut out of school on the day of his accident, right?" Phil's hands are on her hips. She's leaning toward the guys. "I realize you're as loyal as blood brothers, but we need to figure out what happened on Wednesday. When did Joey ditch school?"

Cheets shoots an expression of wide-eyed panic at Jacks. Katz squirms.

Jacks shifts from foot to foot. "Jim Kelley saw Tags leave school after second period."

"Junior took off after second period, too," Katz blurts out.

My eyes roll. These guys buckle way too easy.

"Junior? Chuck Hector?" Phil snarls. "Sam Hector's son?"

Jacks nods.

"Why'd he leave school at the same time as Joey?" Phil's question has an urgent edge.

"I, uh, might have let slip how good Joey is at tracking deer. How Joey can track and find Old Buck." Jacks shrugs. "I forgot about the bet."

Phil jerks. "*Bet?* What bet?"

"Your dad bet Sam that Joey would shoot a buck before Junior did," Katz explains.

"What?" Phil's eyes get huge.

"From what I heard, it wasn't a serious bet," Cheets says. "But Junior's dad took it seriously. So did Tags."

Dad strolls into the room as Phil's lips press together and her jaw clenches. "Hey, everyone," he says.

"Hey, Mr. Tags." Jacks glances from my dad to my sister and then back to Dad. "Philly says that Joey's doing pretty well, considering."

"Yes." Dad offers a polite smile. "Considering." And then he turns to Phil. "Your mom is on her way. She's talking to the Zuckermans." His smile turns real. "She's decided not to go with them to Mexico at the end of this month, but she'll go with them to Arizona in February."

"Fine," Phil says in a flat tone. "But what's this about some hunting bet that you made with Sam Hector?" Phil's voice turns accusing. "Joey thought he had to shoot a deer to come through for you? What's that about?"

The posse squirms. They exchange uncomfortable glances. They shuffle sneakers and boots. Cheets keeps glancing at the doorway. Any minute he'll make a run for it.

I wait for Dad to respond. He blinks, stunned.

"A bet," Phil repeats. "Something you said about Joey being able to shoot a buck." The fact that her tone isn't getting her grounded for life shows that Dad is thrown.

"Er, I think we'd better get going," Jacks says in a trickling voice.

Cheets is already at the door. Katz keeps stealing peeks at his watch.

"Tell Joey we'll come by again tomorrow. Okay?" Jacks escapes without waiting for an answer. Katz isn't far behind. Cheets is already history.

Phil and Dad don't seem to notice the posse bolting. Dad's eyes are wide-open windows to his full-out shock. "Some of my friends were kidding around about taking our kids out hunting for the first time. There were all kinds of playful bets being thrown around about this and that. You know, stupid stuff. Joking around the pool table. Talk and nonsense."

"Well, one of those bets got back to Joey," Phil tells him. "He took it seriously. So did that Sam Hector. Too seriously."

Dad closes his eyes as he shakes his head. "I don't believe this." He sighs. "But everything is starting to make sense."

CHAPTER 15

THURSDAY, THE THIRTEENTH DAY

My foot has been replaced by a mummy's limb. And it's about as useful. I move slow from the gravel and grit of the All-Stars Rink parking lot, where Jeebs and the Minivan of Death dropped me off, to the lobby. The crutches and the pain medication have me teetering, but I'm able to open one of the double glass doors and push my way inside.

No one would believe how much I've missed everything about this place, even the frayed and stringy red rug that smells of mold. I crutch-crawl across it, over to the glass cabinets. Nobody spends much time in this lobby, except to pause here, the way that I'm doing now, and eye the trophies and framed photographs of outstanding players.

It's hard not to stare at my picture, not to think about how different life was when it was taken, the day after I'd sent a slap shot down the ice to score the winning goal of the season last year. I couldn't have connected with that puck any better. It flew right through the goalie's legs in overtime to win the championship.

Back then I didn't think anything could be better than scoring the final goal to win a game, back when I had two good feet and hockey was a given, not a question.

The voices of the players echo out from the huge, oval rink in the center of this building, the heart of this place. I steer my crutches toward it.

"All the hockey games, from the squirt leagues through the adult leagues, get packed with fans that speak hockey lingo as a first language," Phil is saying as she busts through the front doors. "These people consider the good players celebrities, which explains why my little brother gets treated like Wayne Gretzky." Phil crosses the lobby.

Lexi, swinging her six-foot-long, bright purple scarf, a thing with at least a foot of fringe on either end, skips along after my sister.

"Of course, he won't get treated like Wayne Gretzky anymore," Philly adds.

Jeebs, trailing behind Lex, bobs his head. "That's brutal."

No kidding.

"Excuse me, Joey," my sister snaps. She pushes her hair off her pink-flushed face, color left over from cross-country practice. "Didn't I tell you to wait by the front doors?"

I ignore her and crutch-waddle to the second pair of glass doors. I get past them the same way I got by the first pair, to prove that I'm not an invalid.

Sure, Phil is being annoying, but it's hard to stay mad at her after the way that she tried to save me in the woods and get my drawing into the art show. Also, she got Jeebs to drive straight from cross-country practice to Jefferson Middle School to pick me up this afternoon, which saved me from captivity (Mom is making me stay after school for *extra help*). My sister also talked Jeebs into picking up the posse and hauling everyone back to 5 Mercer Place to celebrate my hospital release. And Mom coming home.

Mom is teaching Dad how to make her chicken and mushroom crepes and her salads. A small move that Philly and I have exchanged a few smiles over. Yeah, Mom and Dad have been working together the way they used to do, but this time to carve out new routines. This makes Philly grin extra-big since she won't be expected to do as much the next time Mom travels.

As I head down the sloping aisle, past rows of folding seats, trying to stay upright on scaffolding, my nose takes in the clean chill coming off of the white ice. I imagine being on blades again and gliding across this polished marble surface. Even the heavy-duty pain medication can't numb the adrenaline rush that comes from this fantasy or the ache of not being able to act on it.

The usual spectators, here to watch the hockey practices, try not to stare at me. In return, I try not to show my anger. These days, I'm the bear out of the cave. For now, I try to concentrate on the deep and steady pounding of my heart, which gets quicker as I get closer to the rink.

Skates cut and scrape. Sticks slap pucks and each other. Coach's whistle shrieks. Voices full of enthusiasm bounce off the walls and the high ceiling. All of these sounds echo. I can almost taste the excitement. Every cell in my hands craves the feel of Flyer in my grip.

At the four-foot-high wall topped with shatterproof glass that's supposed to protect spectators from flying pucks and high-sticks, I peer out across the ice. I'm on the wrong side of this divider. Where is my team?

The twelves and thirteens of the Penguin League, thick in their shoulder and elbow pads, shin guards and helmets, are gliding in, out, and around one another. They are working their L-shaped sticks with gloved hands. They are weaving patterns determined by the coach, obeying his orders. Coach Grimes, an ex–pro hockey player somewhere in his middle-age years, is whipping his hands about while chewing an immense wad of gum. He's lecturing a shoulder-slumped Tim Tailor, whose stick is flat on the ice. Yeah, good times.

"In some ways, every one of those players looks like Joey," Phil is telling Jeebs and Lexi as the three of them come up behind me. And then she jabs me with her bony elbow. "But not one of them moves with the same fast slices and quick turns that you did, Little Brother."

Did. My mangled foot throbs. I want to throw my crutches at something.

"Not one of them holds his chin as high as Joey did," Lexi chirps, whirling around in a dance move that she calls a pirouette.

"It's true," Phil agrees. "Little Brother has an attitude. None of those other players has his intensity." She watches them for a minute. "Do they see that you're here?"

Before I can growl that this doesn't matter, Phil shoves her pointer fingers into her mouth and lets out her three-note whistle shriek. Almost every seventh grader slows or stops. Some turn small half-circles to face us. Others whip glances over their shoulders.

Jacks stops the minute he picks out Phil. His cool-guy attitude slides off his mug as if it's been greased. A vibrant purple-red rises up under his freckles. His goofy grin makes him appear insane. He shoots over to us, no longer self-conscious about being skinny, now that he's got the hockey pads on. When he reaches us, he does a two-foot hockey stop. I try not to roll my eyes as the show-off's blades spray ice against the wall.

"Impressive," Phil offers.

Lexi throws up the ends of her scarf. "Bravo!"

Jeebs scratches one of his eyebrows. He's not looking impressed.

"Thanks." Jacks grins at Phil, grips his hockey stick tighter. I'm pretty sure he's trying to flex his muscles under his gear.

I shift on my crutches. "How goes practice?" The question comes out irritable.

Jacks shrugs. "Rough without you, Tags." He shakes his head. "Rough without you."

"Jackson!" The deep voice of Coach Grimes rolls across the rink and bounces off the boards. "You here to chitchat or play hockey?"

"Hockey, sir!" Jacks raises his stick in an exclamation.

"Then get over here!" the coach barks. And then he flips me a brief wave before he turns his attention to Cheets, who is in the goal, barely able to move in all his padding and protective gear.

"Gotta go." Jacks glances back over his shoulder at us. "We're finishing up, though."

I just nod, watching him glide back to our team. Or, his team.

Jacks and Cheets strut ahead of Katz and me, crunch onto the gravel parking lot of the All-Stars Rink. Jacks swings his hockey stick up and over his right shoulder. Then he lets it fly to score an imaginary goal. One more to add to the four real scores at practice—pucks that were black streaks against the white ice. Arrows that went straight into Cheets's net and ruined his afternoon.

Jeebs, Philly, and Lexi are ahead of us, moving toward the van. Phil is growling because I refused to be picked up at the door. Jeebs is humming "Love the One You're With."

Katz, who had a decent practice, holds the door open for me. His free hand clutches a strawberry Pop-Tart. "How'd it feel to watch practice from the stands, Tags?"

"Like crap." I hop through the doorway, nearly fall over. Again. Four days of being on crutches full-time and already this one-legged gig is getting old. Four days since I got out of the hospital on Monday. The tenth day of deer season.

Katz watches me. "When will you be able to play again?"

I head for the van: crutches, good foot, crutches, good foot. "Yesterday, the surgeon said—" My throat closes over the last words. "Maybe never."

Jacks stops dead in the middle of getting off another slap shot. The blade of his hockey stick hangs suspended over his right shoulder as he turns to face me. His jaw drops.

Katz stops chewing the Pop-Tart. He doesn't seem to care that there's a blob of strawberry goo hanging off his bottom lip.

Cheets stops, too. He turns to Katz and me. "What about the Jersey game?"

Jacks aborts his swing. "*Never* means he'll miss that game, Beef for Brains."

Cheets blinks as this sinks in.

Being reminded that I can't be a part of the Jersey game

feels like I got shot through the chest instead of the foot. Still, I keep up my annoying tortoise crawl to the parking lot, trying to stay focused on maintaining my balance. Thinking about everything that I will be missing only makes me more angry. And sad.

Katz lets the door close behind us. "Never?" His question has a tone of disbelief, as if *never* is too big for him to hold on to. Yeah, I get this.

"That surgeon doesn't know crap," I snap. "He doesn't know about my plans. The Hockey Hall of Fame. With you guys." I focus on Jacks. "You and me, Philadelphia Flyers."

He stares at his feet. No one moves.

"That surgeon doesn't know," I yell. But my voice wavers. Any idiot could see the pity on the faces of these guys. "I can't believe you dorks are listening to some stupid doctor." I push ahead on the crutches, trying to go faster. "I can do whatever I want, whenever I want," I spit. "You guys know that."

Jacks comes over to me, but he doesn't look at me. "Sure, Tags, whatever you say." He picks at the tape wrapped around his hockey stick handle. He's too serious. I want his sarcasm. I want him to tell me that I deserve a beating for even thinking about what that stupid surgeon said. I want Jacks, Cheets, and Katz to knock me off these crutches. I want us to get back to normal.

"Junior and his father should pay for what happened to

you," Jacks mutters instead. "Especially Junior. Some friend he turned out to be."

I sigh, come down off furious, and slide into sad. "I'm the one who shot myself," I remind him. "But seriously, if Junior had been in school the past two days, I'd have thanked him."

"For what?" Katz spits. "For setting you up?"

"No." I shake my head. "I'm pretty sure he called 911, reported my accident, and got the police and ambulance to me."

The posse goes quiet. A rare moment of group consideration as we cross the parking lot in a knot, the guys slowing to my crawl.

"Dudes, Junior is denying that he was in those woods," Cheets informs us. "He's telling everyone that his dad saw M. K. Buckner go after Tags, and that Man-Killer was having one of his flashbacks. The Hectors are spreading the rumor that the man started hunting Tags and made Joey shoot himself in the foot."

"It's their story versus mine," I growl.

"Of course they'd blame M. K. Buckner," Jacks adds. "He's the town bogeyman."

"At least Old Buck is still okay," I say.

"That's true," Cheets agrees. "They haven't taken him down yet."

"But I know that they're after him," I add. "Especially now that they know where to find him." The fact that today is the last day that anyone is allowed to shoot an antlered deer means nothing to those Hectors. This makes my hands tighten on the crutches. My teeth grind. "If I hear anything about them spotlighting him—"

"Easy, Tags," Jacks tells me. "Watch your crutches."

Exactly. Crutches. I've never felt as helpless as I do now. I hate this. HATE this! I want to hurl these stupid crutches into the next county. Or at Sam Hector.

"It rots that you can't prove that Junior and his dad were in those woods with traps and flashlights," Katz puts in. "Between the trespassing, the traps, and the evidence of spotlighting, they'd lose their hunting licenses for sure."

"Mrs. D's camera must have fallen out of my pocket," I mutter.

"Tags, man, we combed through those woods. At least four times. We didn't find any camera," Cheets tells me.

"I already told him," Jacks puts in.

"Thanks, guys," I say.

"Yo, Speed Racer," Phil yells over her shoulder. "Slow down before you wreck your other foot."

Katz eyeballs Phil like she's the big, bad wolf.

But I just shake my head at her. "She's lucky she's not within crutch range," I tell the guys. "I've already figured out how to swing one of these babies as accurately as I swing Flyer."

"Nice." Cheets snickers.

"Ah, give Philly a break," Jacks puts in.

"You don't know," I tell him. "Since the shooting, she's been Miss Velcro. Sticking to me. She keeps trying to take my pulse. She makes Jeebs drive me to school." I shake my head again. "My mom and dad say she'll lighten up. She'd better. And soon."

Warden Phil loses her smile and steps up to me as the posse reaches the van. "Did you bring *all* of your books from school?"

Jacks gazes at her in a way that makes me think that he's swallowed a mess of my pain pills.

"You'd better have all of your books in the van, Little Brother," Phil says to me, apparently missing Jacks's crush face. For a straight-A student, she's utterly clueless. "You miss one more minute of school or blow off one more homework assignment, you'll be redoing seventh grade."

I can still hear Mom making a strangled noise deep in her throat when my guidance counselor shared this piece of news with my parents and me, the day after I got out of the hospital. Mom covered her mouth with both of her hands. Dad put his arm around her. I'd refused to redo seventh grade. That left only one option.

"Your tutor is coming tomorrow morning," Phil adds.

I roll my eyes. "Thanks for the announcement." It's bad enough that I've got one less toe, can't play hockey, and have a future of Saturday mornings with stupid tutors. I don't need my sister's brand of nagging on top of all this. Bottom line: It's not true what I tell the guys. What I tell everyone. I *don't* feel fine.

Katz focuses on me. "A tutor, Tags?"

Jacks groans. He knows I don't need the whole, stinking mess broadcasted.

"To make up for the classes I've missed." Or messed up in. Or spent too much time drawing in. Whatever.

I lift myself into the van and slide in beside Lex. She grabs my crutches for me. "I'm in for summer school, too," I tell the guys. And then I reach for my hearing aid to turn down the volume, in preparation for the posse cackle-laughter.

"Summer school? Dude, that's brutal." Cheets doesn't come close to snickering.

"Yeah." It's all I can say. I'm melting into this unexpected sympathy. My right hand drops without touching the hearing aid.

"Summer school beats redoing seventh grade, though." Jacks climbs in next to me.

How did I forget that I can always count on him to back me up? In more ways than one.

Jeebs starts up the van. It's louder than a herd of buffalo with bad gas.

"Man, Tags, you've had a rotten week," Jacks says over the noise of the van.

"It could have been worse," Phil tells us as Jeebs steers

the van-beast out of the parking lot. "He could have died in those woods."

"I would have if I hadn't been rescued," I say.

"Don't start with that again." Jacks shakes his head. "I told you, I'm not buying your theory about Man-Killer Buckner saving your sorry butt, Tags."

Katz busts out in a snorting laugh. "Yeah, come on, Tags. M. K. Buckner carrying you out of the woods? What kind of heavy medication did those doctors put you on?"

"A big guy hauled me out of Dewey's woods," I growl through gritted teeth.

"Is it true, Philly?" Jacks turns to her.

She shrugs as she smears on pink lip gloss. "Someone or something saved Joey's scrawny butt from bleeding to death."

Cheets snickers. "Dude, your butt was bleeding?" Mr. Mature.

Phil ignores Cheets. "For all I know, the Jolly Green Giant could have saved Joey's carcass. The big guy didn't stick around long enough for me to talk to him."

"That Buckner dude knows those woods better than anyone," Cheets says. "You know, from spending all his nights in there, stalking prey. People say he learned how to pick up on the scent of fresh blood while he was in Vietnam and that this is how he tracks wounded victims." Cheets glances at me then. "Others say the raw odor of the blood sends him into flashbacks. If M. K. found you, Tags, he'd have snuffed you, man." Cheets draws a finger across his throat, as if slitting it with a blade. "Is that intense or what?"

"An intense pile of cow crap." I roll my eyes. "Where'd you get that from? Junior?"

Cheets shrugs.

"Whoever the guy was, the cops seemed to know him," Philly cuts in.

"Wild," Jeebs mutters.

"It was M. K. Buckner," I tell everyone.

I wish I could prove it.

CHAPTER 16

THURSDAY, THE LAST DAY

No one utters a word as the minivan sputters toward the Buckner place.

"Stop," I tell Jeebs.

He plants his foot hard on the brakes. The van takes its time slowing.

Philly whips around in her seat to glare at me. "Why do you want to stop?"

I stare at the Victorian house. Part of me wants some sign from M. K., an answer to all my questions. Did he haul me out of Dewey's woods? If yes, how did he find me? Was he looking for me? Or was he in the woods already?

Jacks stiffens. "You see that?" One of his fingers goes rigid, points at the Buckner house.

Phil's eyes grow big. "I saw it," she whispers.

Jeebs mashes his face up to the windshield. "Aww, I didn't see anything."

Lexi pulls her scarf over her face and tucks her head between her knees.

I turn up the volume on my hearing aid. "Let me out."

"The curtain moved, right?" Philly stares at Jacks. "In the window beside the front door."

Before he can answer, the van door opens. I shove him, along with Katz and Cheets, toward the sidewalk.

"The curtain did move," Katz answers Philly once he's out of the van. His voice cracks.

"That's not cool," Cheets mutters, plastering his back up against the side of the van.

I crawl out, grab my crutches. No one speaks as I position the sticks under my arms. But Cheets about chokes on his own tongue when I hobble over to the black metal gate. For once there's no thick chain threaded through it, holding it to the fence. There's no padlock.

"Tags, what are you doing?" Jacks sounds freaked.

"Joey, get back here," Phil snaps as she throws herself out of the van.

I push open the gate with my right crutch.

"Check out the little man," Jeebs says as he comes around the front of his van.

"Dude, stay away from the porch steps. He buried his mother under them," Cheets says, trying to keep his voice low.

"Are you crazy? Out of your mind?" Katz's voice hits the whine zone.

"Are you squawking like a girl?" I keep heading up the walkway without looking back. I sound tough, but I'm sweating big-time. As I get to the porch steps, my nose recognizes fresh paint and new wood. My heart pounds harder.

Cheets gasps. "The curtain totally moved again!"

I stop. Yeah, I saw it, too. A flutter of green in the window to the right of the door.

A bolt slides back with a heavy metal clunk. Doorknob metal grinds. The front door cracks open. Classical music seeps out from the dark. A big hand follows and drifts down to the porch floor. Long, thick fingers slide a silver camera over to me.

Katz screams. "Hit the ground! Dive! Dive!"

Leaning forward, somehow not falling off the crutches, I grab the camera. My heart is thumping hard enough to crack a few ribs. "No way," I breathe. "Mrs. D's camera."

I look up at the darkness between the door and the doorjamb. The hand has disappeared. "Thanks," I say into the shadows. "For the camera." I glance at my bandaged foot. Then back at the dark space. "And for getting me out of the woods."

The door doesn't move. But I know someone's behind it—someone big and broad who smells of cigarettes and bubble gum.

After a long minute, the door closes in slow motion. The doorknob and bolt mechanisms click. I wish they hadn't. Because I know, now, that M. K. does not stand for Man-Killer. But who is this guy? Does he hunt? Has he seen Old Buck?

But the door stays closed.

After a minute, I slip the loop of the camera handle around my wrist. And then I turn in hops. Twelve wide eyes are staring at me. Six jaws are hanging open. I start toward them.

"Did you see that?" Cheets sounds like he's going to wet himself.

I stump toward them as if getting close to a reclusive, rumored-lunatic war veteran is no big deal. But I glance back at the house every couple steps.

"You were within inches of Man-Killer Buckner." Jacks's voice is full of awe.

As if I don't know this. "Just so you chumps know: There's no body buried under those porch steps." I go through the gate opening. I am nowhere near rushing.

"You're my hero," Jacks mutters. "But you're insane."

"Whatever. I got this." I lift the camera, glance at the Buckner house again. Is he watching?

"Maybe M. K. Buckner did haul you out of those woods, Tags," Katz says.

"Intense," Cheets mutters.

"Let me see that." Phil almost knocks me over as she grabs the camera. The strap bites into my wrist as she pulls. I slip my hand free because I can't fight her and stay vertical.

She turns the camera over again and again, starts poking at buttons. Lexi crawls out of the van to check this out. "Okay, we got pictures of a deer with horns here," Phil says, staring into the LCD screen.

I roll my eyes. "They're called antlers. And that's not any deer. That's Old Buck."

"Whoa, impressive," Jeebs mutters, peering over Phil's shoulder.

"There's Sam Hector with a gun and a beer." Philly shifts the camera to let Jacks, Cheets, and Katz glimpse the screen.

I hop closer to the camera.

"You took some awesome pictures before shooting yourself in the foot, Little Brother."

Of course Phil jumps at the opportunity to highlight my idiot move. As if I don't understand the price I'm paying for not following Dad's rules.

"We've got to get these pictures to the police," she adds. "And then—"

"Hello," Mrs. D chirps as she crosses the street, coming toward us.

Everyone turns to the woman wearing her husband's barn coat and black, rubber ankle boots with oversize wool socks poking out of the top of them.

"Hey, Mrs. D." I eye the golden-crusted pie in her hands, which is covered in plastic wrap. I think I smell blueberries. "Look!" I point at her camera.

She moves to clap her hands and almost drops the pie. And then she glances at the Buckner house before looking back at me. "Did Michael Buckner give you that? He said that he had something for you, but I had no idea that he meant my camera."

I blink at her. "Mrs. D," I mutter in a tone of hushed awe. "You talked to M. K. Buckner?"

"Yes, of course." She smiles. "I speak with him all the time. My husband and I were friends with Dorothy and Harold Buckner. I've been keeping an eye on Michael since Dorothy's passing. I've done shopping for him and have run errands for him." She sighs. "He loves homemade pies. Dorothy used to bake them for him often. Pies remind him of his childhood, a more peaceful, innocent time for him." She blinks. "He was a different person before his tours in Vietnam. Believe it or not, he was outgoing, social, and friendly. But he's lived through too much. It's affected him." She shakes her head.

I gawk at her with my mouth hanging open. So does the posse.

"He thought that you'd come up to the house to thank him for pulling you out of the woods. After all, you were brave enough to approach his house when the window got smashed."

I stop breathing. Everyone stiffens. Jaws drop. Jacks, Katz, and Cheets do their best impressions of zombies.

"When Michael saw the Hectors following you, he tracked them." She smiles, tips her head, watching me take this in. "He knows those woods as well as you do, Joey. Mr. Dewey has let Michael on that property for years, although he doesn't hunt much. Not since Vietnam."

"M. K. turned out to be a better man than Junior," Jacks mutters.

Katz and Cheets just stare at the Victorian house.

Mrs. D glances at her pie. "I don't think Michael knows about the pictures that you took, Joey, but I'm sure he would agree that it's time for Sam Hector to be held accountable for his actions." She looks up at me. "The police know Michael, trust that he went into those woods to help you, but people gossip about him. They listen to stories. Michael doesn't need the stress of people blaming him for what has happened to you."

She boot-shuffles toward the black gate. "Well, it's been a trying week. Michael could use a pie." On the other side of the gate she starts along the walkway to the house, but pauses one more time to glance back at me. "Use the camera to prove to people who was poaching the day of your accident, Joey. Make sure folks understand that Michael was in the woods to help, not to hurt." Mrs. D offers a mild smile before she starts toward the Buckner house again.

Phil turns on the balls of her sneakers to face Jeebs and

Lex. "Mrs. Davies is right. Let's get this camera to the police station, now."

Jeebs lifts his keys. "Your wish is my command, Princess!"

"Thanks anyway, Phil." I lean toward her, balanced, and take back the camera. "But I want to be the one that pays back Michael Buckner."

As Mrs. D hums, sounding pleased, my father's truck pulls up to the curb. Before anyone moves, the passenger's side window slides down. The aroma of tangy tomato, baked crust, and cheese floats out on warm air. "Everybody hungry?" Dad grins big. No more puffy, sleep-deprived eyes for him. No more razor-stubble grit. He's still wearing his leather jacket. "I kind of messed up your mom's chicken dish, so we're having pizza." He shrugs, chuckles. "But don't worry, I'm not giving up on learning how to cook. And I have mastered the salads." He winks.

Katz leans toward the back window of the truck. His eyes zero in on the stack of white pizza boxes stamped with red print. "Pepperoni?" He practically drools on himself.

For once pizza doesn't hold my attention. I straighten between the crutches. "Dad, I've got Mrs. D's camera." I hold it up as if it's a grand prize.

His face brightens. "Great! That's what the police need. But how did you get—" He glances at the Buckner house. "Ah, okay. Get in the truck, son. Let's run that camera over to the police station."

Phil is at my side in a blink. She opens the passenger's side door and grabs at my crutches, trying to help me into the truck. I wave her away as if she's a gnat, but as usual, this does no good.

"Philly." Dad throws a thumb at the rear of the truck. "Why don't you grab the pizzas, bring them to the house. Your brother and I will meet you-all there."

Phil hesitates, but then moves to the back of the truck. Dad winks at me. I mouth a thanks. He snaps off a salute.

The second Phil wraps her hands around the pizza boxes, Katz dives at her with outstretched arms. "Let me help you with those."

Cheets grunts. "Trusting him with pizza is like trusting a shark with a swimmer."

Meanwhile, Jeebs circles around to the back of his van, lifts the back door, and starts raking aside his dog-eared paperbacks and worn notebooks to make space for the pizzas.

Once the transfer has been made, the posse (minus me), Philly, Lex, and Jeebs all pile back into the van. As it rumbles, blowing explosions of air, Dad shakes his head. "Your mother and I are going to have to talk about whether you and your sister are going to be allowed to ride in that thing anymore."

Before Mom came home, this threat would have been weightless. Not now, with Mom and Dad talking, being a team again.

Dad turns the key in the ignition. The truck roars to life. My fingers curl over the camera, protective, as I watch Mrs. D climb the porch steps. "Dad, you know who carried me out of those woods, don't you?"

He rubs his forehead, sucks in a long breath. "Yes. And I'll be forever grateful to him."

The Buckner house remains still as Mrs. D crosses the porch with her pie.

"M. K. Buckner is a human version of Old Buck, isn't he, Dad?" Bigger in myth than in real life. Content to be what he is.

And maybe this is how I should be—content to be what I am.

"That's not a bad comparison, son. Michael needs to get to know someone before he can trust that person. Like Old Buck, apparently."

As Mrs. D opens the front door, I hold my breath, hoping. But there are no more signs of M. K. Buckner. Until—Did a curtain move again in a window? As Dad pulls the truck away from the curb, a hand moves close to the glass, sways back and forth in a shy wave.

Pressing myself against the truck door, I return a wave. And I smile inside and out, until the big hand pulls back and disappears.

Dad places his own palm flat on my knee. "Taking those pictures with that camera was smart thinking, son. And brave. Too brave for your own good, but I'm proud of you."

His hand moves to my shoulder. He jiggles it in a playful move that feels like the old us.

Proud. Not a word that comes out of Dad's mouth often.

I swallow. I straighten as best as I can. Flushed with a new confidence, I call up courage that I didn't have a week ago. "Will you still be proud of me if I don't go hunting again?"

Dad's expression slides into cool neutral. He stares at the road for a long time. His Adam's apple moves up and then down. "Yes," he says after about ten years. "Yes, of course, I'll still be proud of you."

As I absorb this, he reaches for the brown bag of jelly beans on the dashboard. He pours rainbow colors into his palm and tosses them into his mouth. And then he pushes the open bag to me in an offering that I don't think he's ever made before. My hand moves with caution. My fingers carefully scoop multicolored beans.

Dad chews, looking thoughtful, and then he swallows. "Joey, I want to apologize to you for making that stupid bet. It never meant anything." He glances at me. His eyes glisten before he turns his attention back to the road. "I wanted hunting to teach you responsibility and respect for nature. Maybe even life in general. But now I see that you've been learning all of this all along."

I try to toss the jelly beans and catch them in my mouth the way he does. A couple of them go in. A few others bounce off my teeth.

"You and I are father and son no matter what," Dad continues. "Drawings or no drawings, hunting or no hunting, buck or no buck, bet or no bet."

"Yeah, I know, Dad," I say after I swallow. And for the first time I do know.

EPILOGUE

It's the perfect day to be in Dewey's woods. Crisp, but with plenty of warm sunshine soaking the meadow, offering me the perfect amount of light. The birds are chattering and the trees are whispering, but otherwise all is quiet. My butt rests on the stone wall. My crutches lean against it. Everything I need is within my reach.

Old Buck is grazing, pulling at freeze-dried grasses, enjoying, I think, the December sun on his thick gray-brown fur. He stands broadside to me, his cloven hooves stepping only as he moves from one patch of grass to another. Once in a while he lifts his head to watch me, but never with concern.

I wait for him to take another step, to get into range. He does. Without breathing, moving only as much as I have to, I set up my shot. This is almost too easy. Old Buck is in perfect view. *Steady,* I whisper to myself. *Don't rush this, don't startle him.* I line him up, adjust my aim. *Don't blow this.*

Click.

I don't even bother to check the LCD screen. I know that I got a great shot. I can feel it. Besides, there will be plenty of other opportunities to take more pictures of Old Buck.

So I put down Mrs. D's camera, pick up the sketch pad and one of the pencils. My fingers guide the charcoal point to where I need to add more shading. I think. I'll have to ask Mrs. D. Maybe tonight when she comes over to our house for dinner. Dad is making meat loaf. My parents invited her over to talk about what kind of art lessons I should be taking. Once I get my grades up.

A breeze rattles the tree limbs, shuffles the bushy evergreens. Old Buck lifts his head, still chewing, alert for signs of danger. The way he holds his head up, his rack of twelve points high in the air, makes him look even more proud, strong, and regal. A handsome example of a whitetail buck. The white markings around his eyes and nose, and even the scar across his face, add to this look but also show that he's not a young deer. He's been around awhile. He's managed to survive despite the world that he lives in.

The way M. K. Buckner has.

Again I put down my pad and pencils. I lift the camera. I aim, line up Old Buck, and fire off another shot. And then another.

ACKNOWLEDGMENTS

I would like to offer my heartfelt thanks to the following people for their many contributions to this novel:

My husband, Bill, who made this book possible with his incredibly valuable perspectives, expertise, guidance, informative connections, and endless patience. "Thank you" is simply not big enough.

Steven Chudney of The Chudney Agency. His advice, direction, and encouragement helped this book come into being.

Liz Szabla, my brilliant editor, who guided me into bringing out the best in this story with her amazing insights. And, extra-special thanks to all the talented, wonderful folks at Feiwel and Friends.

Karen S. Brady, R.N., who took the time to share her medical expertise and answer all of my questions with precision and detail.

Robyn Ulmer, Esta Schwartz, and everyone at the Barnes and Noble in Bridgewater, New Jersey, for their continued support and encouragement. And for their love of books.

Thank you for reading
this FEIWEL AND FRIENDS book.

The Friends who made

BUCK FEVER

possible are:

Jean Feiwel, publisher
Liz Szabla, editor-in-chief
Rich Deas, creative director
Elizabeth Fithian, marketing director
Holly West, assistant to the publisher
Dave Barrett, managing editor
Nicole Liebowitz Moulaison, production manager
Jessica Tedder, associate editor
Caroline Sun, publicist
Allison Remcheck, editorial assistant
Ksenia Winnicki, marketing assistant
Kathleen Breitenfeld, designer